Also by Eric Praschan

Therapy for Ghosts

SLEEPWALKING INTO DARKNESS

A Novel

ERIC PRASCHAN

Sleepwalking into Darkness. Copyright © 2013 Eric Praschan
All rights reserved. No part of this book may be used or reproduced in any manner whatsoever without written permission, except in the case of brief quotations embodied in critical articles and reviews.

This book is a work of fiction. Names, characters, places, and incidents either are products of the author's imagination or are used fictitiously. Any resemblance to actual events or locales or persons, living or dead, is entirely coincidental.

ISBN-13: 978-0988174733
ISBN-10: 0988174731

Visit www.amazon.com to order additional copies.

For Judy Praschan,
the greatest mother a son could hope for.

Acknowledgements

I owe a debt of gratitude to Sandy Vekasy for her inspiration, encouragement, friendship, and editing prowess. To my family—your tireless support sustains me. A special thanks to my CoMo Crew for parties, potlucks, love, and laughter.

SLEEPWALKING INTO DARKNESS

PART ONE:
Slumber

Cindy James

A handsome man's face haunts my blurry vision, lowering to kiss my forehead.

"Good morning, Sunshine. Hope you feel better," says Tony, with a sympathetic smile.

"I can make it," I say, coughing into the crook of my elbow.

He pats my arm and looms over me. The congestion in my nose doesn't allow me to take in the normally comforting scent of his cologne. I survey his olive eyes, high cheekbones, and narrow nose. Rogue gray patches have invaded his light brown hair, but, even so, his profile hasn't lost its appeal to me. He is aging well—far better than I am.

"You can make it as far as the bathroom," he says. "I'll be fine on my own. Please stop fighting, and accept the fact that you're sick."

I sigh. "I'm not sick. I'm just not feeling well." Another hacking fit erupts into my elbow. "I'm sorry I won't be there."

He grins and removes a piece of lint from the lapel of his black pinstripe suit. "I'd rather be bed-ridden here with you. It's only an interview with *Psychology Today*. Nothing special."

I shake my head. "Don't minimize it. This is your big opportunity."

He leans down and pecks my cheek. "I'll feel your phlegm-filled support from afar. Well, I need to go. I have people waiting to pick my brain."

"Good luck," I say.

He smiles and circles around the bed. "Thanks. By the way, something came for you in today's mail. It's a little strange. I left it on your nightstand. See you tonight."

He disappears through the doorway. I glance around the bedroom, as the tiny rays of Arkansas sunshine peek in through the edges of the closed light brown curtain. The cream-colored walls, teal and tan bedspread, and various nature portraits framed on the walls—capturing all four seasons—usually offer me a sense of calm first thing in the morning, but they have no such effect today. Half a minute passes before the front door closes downstairs. The hum of Tony's red Ford Taurus easing down the driveway to his advancing career soothes my ears.

I reach to the nightstand for the bottle of cough syrup, but I change my mind and grasp the "strange" item Tony left for me—a pink envelope with no return address and no stamp, just my name written on the front in cursive letters. I turn over the envelope, undo the seal, and retrieve a piece of small white paper. As I scan the words scrawled in eerily familiar handwriting, I feel my face losing color.

Dear Cindy,
There is so much I never told you because it wasn't safe. Now it's time for you to know. Look in the chess set. What you do with it is up to you, but I trust you'll make the right decision.
Love,
Mama

I glance to the corner of the room, where a marble chess set sits atop an end table beside a rocking chair. Oddly, an old stranger revisits my mind. A fuzzy image of Mama and me sitting on the wooden floor of the mansion library. Her black hair has unusually playful curls, offsetting her pale, pleasant face, which is no longer purple with bruises. The marble chess set sits between us, half of its finely chiseled pieces still on the board, the others lying to the side.

"What do you think we should do for your birthday, Cindy?" asks Mama, moving a knight ahead two spaces and then one across.

I shrug and slide my rook ahead six spots, taking out her bishop. "I don't know, Mama. A cake or something, I guess."

Mama smiles. "Fifteen is an important year." Then she lowers her voice. "Maybe we can leave the house and go somewhere fun."

I stare at her, aghast. "We can't do that, Mama. You know Grandma's rules."

She bites her lower lip. "Yes, I know, but it's your birthday. We should do something special."

I grow excited against my better judgment. "Really? You think we actually can?"

She pats my leg. "I'll see what I can do."

"I can't wait!" I say, trying in vain to whisper.

Mama inches her queen into an open square. "Did I ever tell you why this chess set is so special to the family?"

I shake my head and find a new spot for my other knight. "No. Grandma said something about it two years ago when we first moved in, but I've never heard anything since then."

"Well, it's very important because—"

"Cindy, come here right this minute!" Grandma's commanding voice ricochets throughout the five levels of the house.

Both Mama and I flinch. My knee knocks against the chessboard and sends the pieces scattering across the floor.

"Coming, Grandma!" I yell.

I look at Mama, seeing sadness in her expression.

"You better run along," she says. "You don't want to disappoint her."

I nod and stand to my feet. "Sorry, Mama."

"What for?" she asks.

I point to the chess mess below. "For knocking over the pieces, and for having to go."

She clambers to her feet and hauls me in for a hug. Her voice is a strained whisper. "Never apologize for how things are in this house. It's not your fault. And the chess set, well, let's just say it's not what's on top of the board that's important. Always remember that. I love you."

Then she kisses my forehead. I separate from her and race out of the library toward the sound of Grandma's voice still echoing in my ears.

The memory flash disappears.

Blinking, I find myself back in my bedroom, staring at the chess set. I have not had that memory before. Mama never finished telling me why the chess set was important to our family. Perhaps she forgot to explain it later, or perhaps Grandma interfered. I also remember that we were never able to do anything special for my birthday. At the time, that reality stung more than not hearing Mama's secret about the chessboard.

    I glance at the note in my hands scribbled in her unmistakable handwriting, while hearing her voice resonating in my mind: "Let's just say it's not what's on top of the board that's important." My curiosity is too strong. I snag a pair of scissors from the nightstand drawer, crawl out of bed, and head to the well-worn, dark brown rocking chair beside the chess set. My white nightgown clings to me as I move. After slumping down and fending off another barrage of coughs, I run my finger along the edge of the chessboard. The smooth surface shows little wear from the decades of usage. I scan the top of the board, finding nothing out of place, nothing questionable.

    Before I can reconsider, I grip both sides of the board and tip it at an angle. The black and white pieces clink in my ears as they collide with one another before bouncing against the cream-colored carpet. Turning over the board, I find a rubber insert covering the underside. I remember Mama explaining that she had the rubber insert added when the two of us started playing chess on a weekly basis in the mansion library. Grandma would, as Mama used to say with a snicker, "breathe dragon fire" if she ever found the spotless wooden floor scratched from our gaming episodes, so the rubber backing would at least give Grandma one less reason to seek us out for discipline and judgment.

    I trace the rubber lining with my fingertips, marveling at its staying quality all these years. Mama's words reverberate within me like a ringing bell: "Let's just say it's not what's on top of the board that's important." As I wedge the scissor blades between the rubber rim and the bottom lip of the marbled edge, my heartbeat spikes with anticipation. A coating of superglue connects the rubber to the board. My fog of sickness seems to suspend while I use the scissor blades to slice away at the glue barrier until I can peel the protective covering from the chessboard.

    Inside the quarter-inch-wide cavity hides a faded white envelope, labeled *For Cindy*. I set the chessboard onto the floor and open the envelope to remove its contents: two postcards, a 3 x 5 photograph, a letter, and a silver key. I do not recognize the blonde-haired young child in the photo. She is smiling and extending both hands forward, as if ready to be picked up. The back of the photo is in Mama's handwriting: *FIND HER AND SAVE HER.* With trembling hands, I place the photograph and key onto my lap to examine the postcards and letter.

The first postcard shows mountains and is labeled "The Ozark Mountains." The second has only a single peak, "Lookout Mountain." I turn over each card and read in silence. Then I read the letter. My breathing quickens. Clutching the items to my chest, I hurry downstairs, struggling to steady my careening heartbeat.

Lexi James

    I should probably tell Mama about my dark dreams, but I'm sure she would never understand me. No use trying to bring it up in conversation with her. I'll sketch the bizarre ghostly women standing around the gravestone in my notepad tonight, just like I always do. I wish I could talk to Mama about it, but I don't want to worry her.

    I enter the house and listen for Mama's footsteps, but all is quiet. I tiptoe up the stairs to my room, not wanting to wake her since she seemed sick this morning when I left. I rub my wrists together, scraping the already chaffed skin. After kicking off my black high heels, I inspect my room for a moment. Everything is untidy—just as I left it. In the closet, pants, t-shirts, and underwear are scattered about. The bookcase and desk look like the aftermath of an Arkansas twister that tossed papers this way and that, flinging pencils, pens, markers, and paint brushes as if they were bits of straw. I sniff for the scent of Febreze odor remover, but only the whiff of my unwashed clothes fills my nostrils. Mama definitely hasn't been in here today.

    Satisfied with the wreckage, I turn to leave, habitually rolling my eyes at the glossy pink walls. Why Mama insisted on that gaudy, overly-cheery color, I'll never know. No girl wants that much pink in her life—it's not realistic. I know Mama means well, but someday I'll choose my own color, my own room, and my own house. Someday.

    I pause in front of the tall oval mirror beside my dresser, scowling at the thick black curls that I can never straighten to my satisfaction. Mama says my skin is fair, but I consider it pale, almost ghostly. The freckles make me cute, she says, but I only see them as unsightly blotches. In the maroon, long-sleeved dress shirt and black slacks, my bony body looks better than normal, but it still leaves a lot to be desired.

I leave my bedroom and inch my way downstairs, careful not to make a sound. I enter the kitchen, taking in the sight of the spotless black kitchen appliances and the silver pots and pans hanging from a rack above the island in the center of the kitchen. I'm surprised to find Mama sitting on the barstool at the island. She is staring at a pink envelope, two postcards, a photograph, a letter, and a silver key. I make my way across the white linoleum floor toward her.

Suddenly, she looks at me.

"Hi—Mama—" I say, startled.

"Hi, honey. Were you able to find a job for the summer?"

While I mull over the best way to deliver my answer, I notice her unkempt, black, curly hair and fair-skinned round face. I catch myself marveling at her beauty, hoping, as always, that I'll grow into her good looks someday. She wears her white robe and her body slumps over as if too tired to hold itself upright. Yet her eyes sparkle with something I rarely see: fire. She sometimes has that crazy-eyes expression when she's paranoid about the house's being clean or when she's uptight about the possibility of my having a boyfriend in the next twenty years. But I've never seen it quite like this before, this is a side of her I don't know.

"A job?" I stammer. "No. There's nothing available that I want to do. I didn't think it'd be this hard to find something."

"It's all right," she says. "You've only been a high school graduate for two weeks now. You can afford to be patient."

I smile. "I guess so."

She taps her fingers on the two postcards. "Besides, if you don't find what you want, then we can spend more time together."

I chew on my lower lip for a moment. "Sure. Are you feeling better?"

She grins. "Much better."

An awkward pause freezes between us like a frightened rabbit.

"That's good, Mama."

The awkward rabbit-pause makes one hop and then disappears.

She beckons to me. "Come here. I want to show you something."

I plop down on the other barstool. "What's up?"

"We're going to take a trip this summer."

I raise an eyebrow. "Really? Where?"

She smiles with mischief, the same way Daddy does when he has a secret. "I found something important."

I reach out to touch the items on the countertop, but her hand intercepts my fingers and places them at a safe distance. She shakes her head, letting me know these things are off-limits.

"Why are you acting weird, Mama? What's going on?"

She purses her lips. "We've always been a happy family, right?"

I scrunch my forehead in confusion. "Of course."

"And you've always known me as 'normal'? Neurotic, yes, but relatively normal?"

I lean forward, my body tensing. I pick at my eyebrows, tearing some hairs loose. "You're scaring me, Mama. Why are you asking me these questions?"

"Please, honey, just answer me," she says anxiously. "Haven't I always been a good mama to you?"

I give her sweaty hand a squeeze. "Yes, you've been wonderful. You drive me crazy, but I know I do the same to you. Do you need to lie down? Are you still feeling sick?"

She shakes her head. "I'm fine. Don't worry about me."

"Too late, Mama. Please tell me what's going on."

She releases a sigh. "I wasn't always like this—neurotic but relatively normal. There was a time when I was—well—not so normal. You know how your daddy and I told you we met during counseling?"

"Yes," I say, my voice quivering. "You told me you were having stress issues and he helped you."

She offers a sad smile. "That's true, but the circumstances were different than we explained to you. In fact, there are many things we've never shared with you. We wanted to wait until you were old enough to understand. Today, I found these items inside the chessboard. I wasn't ready to tell you everything, but now, after finding these items, I need to share my real story."

"What do you mean, Mama?"

She grimaces. "Promise me something, Lexi."

"Anything, Mama."

"Promise me that you'll try not to think of me differently after I tell you my story."

I see the pain in her expression. Questions ricochet through my mind. "I promise."

The words seem to calm her, at least for the moment. "I wasn't raised in Little Rock, Arkansas, as you've always thought. I was actually born in Chattanooga, Tennessee, and my mama's name was Lisa. She was a wonderful, sweet woman who married a terrible man named Curtis Young. He was abusive, and we lived in fear for a long time, until one day we decided to escape."

***

Over the course of the next four hours, Mama tells me a bizarre story, the kind of dark tale I thought only existed in gothic mystery novels. Mama recounted the poverty and abuse of her childhood in Chattanooga. Her daddy beat her mama, Lisa, for several years. One day Lisa fought back, stabbing him and escaping with my mama to Sleepy Oak, Missouri, where they lived with Elaine, my mama's grandma, in a five-story mansion.

Elaine fascinated me—she seemed like one crazy old bird. Mama found out that Elaine had killed her two previous husbands and lost most of her marbles along the way. It seems that Elaine also tried to come between my mama and Lisa while they lived in the mansion. After Elaine died of a brain tumor, my mama had a rocky relationship with Lisa and left home after high school. She lived in Kansas City for a while, attended college and graduate school, and became a cognitive behavioral therapist. Lisa then became mentally unstable, just like Elaine had. Lisa eventually died of cancer, but Mama moved back to Sleepy Oak to care for her in her last year of life. Between the grief of losing Lisa and the mental instability of the James women creeping into her head, Mama attempted suicide. Thank God she failed.

Many years later, Mama, who was now a therapist, started to have strange panic attacks that triggered recollections of her childhood, which her memory had completely suppressed. She was a psychiatrist's dream (or maybe nightmare): carrying a headless Raggedy Ann doll through the mansion at night, crying herself to sleep in her old bedroom that she had painted red during a nervous breakdown when she also destroyed most of the household possessions, and spot cleaning every square inch of the thirty-one rooms in the mansion with chronic precision like an OCD poster child. In the midst of this, in swept my daddy, the new therapist in town, and they started a doctor-patient relationship to help her recover her memory. Subsequently, they crossed the doctor-patient boundary into romance. Leave it to my parents to be unethical in love.

Once Mama had recovered her memory, she knew she needed to move on with her life. She's always had a flair for the dramatic, so she decided what better way to move on than to burn down the mansion, move to Little Rock, Arkansas, get married to my daddy, and give birth to me? Nothing like a little traumatic family history to spice up my summer vacation.

***

When Daddy arrives home after Mama's four-hour family saga, she and I are still sitting side by side on the island barstools, engrossed in conversation. He casts a suspicious glance our way as he places his briefcase and a large brown bag on the counter.

"I picked up Chinese," he says, his tone raised the way it always is when he senses trouble.

"So, what did they say?" asks Mama.

He grins. "They want me to be a feature writer starting in the fall. I have the rest of the summer to come up with a series of articles."

Mama beams. "Congratulations, honey."

"Good job, Daddy," I say.

He nods. "Thanks. Now, what's with the two of you? This looks dangerous. What are you plotting?"

Mama smiles and lays a hand on my arm. "I was just telling Lexi how you and I met. The real version."

He appears alarmed. "You told her *everything*?"

Mama nods. "Yes, everything. Grandma Elaine. Mama Lisa. My health issues and memory therapy. It's time for her to know."

Daddy watches me anxiously. "Are you okay?"

I shrug. "It explains a lot."

"You're not overwhelmed?" he asks, stepping forward, unsure whether to console me or give me room to process.

I smile. "I'm fine, Daddy. It's a lot to take in, but I'm just glad Mama's all right now."

"Good," he says, appearing relieved. Then he glances at Mama. "So, why is it time for her to know *today* of all days?"

"Pass out the Chinese food," says Mama, "and I'll let you both in on the secret."

"Now you really have me curious," he says.

Within minutes, we are busy making the food disappear. Daddy has pulled a chair from the kitchen table to join us at the island. The strong scents of sesame, orange, and sweet and sour chicken drift into our noses. We all ditch the chopsticks and attack the food with forks. The sound of forks and knives cutting chicken and scraping against plates echoes in my ears, causing me to wince every few minutes. Between mouthfuls, Mama reads the note from the pink envelope.

"'*Dear Cindy, there is so much I never told you because it wasn't safe. Now it's time for you to know. Look in the chess set. What you do with it is up to you, but I trust you'll make the right decision. Love, Mama.*'"

Daddy sets his fork down. "Just one problem. Your mom has been dead for almost thirty years."

Mama offers a nervous laugh. "Exactly. So who wrote this note, and who sent it?"

"Do you think it's a joke?" I ask, hoping the question won't upset her. "Maybe a prank of some kind?"

She nods. "I thought about that, but it's her handwriting. I'm positive. And the items in the chessboard have her handwriting on them as well. It doesn't make any sense."

Daddy scratches his chin. "How did the board come into the family?"

"I don't know," says Mama.

"Would anyone else know there might be something inside it?" asks Daddy.

Mama shakes her head. "There can't be anyone else involved. This is all from my mama."

A grin crosses Daddy's mouth. "So your mom is writing letters to you from beyond the grave?"

Mama glares at him. "There has to be a logical explanation."

Daddy picks up his fork and stabs a piece of chicken. "Show us the items that were hidden inside the chessboard. Maybe we can find a clue."

Mama passes the picture of the blonde-haired girl around for us to peruse.

"'*Find her and save her*'?" Daddy reads from the backside of the photo. "Do you know who she is?"

Mama shrugs. "No clue. All of the women in my family have dark, curly hair. Maybe she was a friend of Grandma Elaine's or my mama's."

I swallow another piece of sweet and sour chicken. "Why do you think Grandma Lisa hid these things in the chessboard?"

Mama grows sad. "It was the only item she knew I would keep from the mansion. Your Grandma Lisa and I used to play our games on it. It was one of the only good times I had as a child. Your Great-Grandma Elaine never touched the chessboard for some reason, so my mama knew she wouldn't look there—it would be safe until I found it."

Daddy hands the photo back to Mama and takes another bite. "What's the key for?"

"No idea," says Mama.

Daddy glances from Mama to the postcards. "So, what do the postcards and the letter say?"

Now Mama's eyes flash with the fire I saw when I first arrived home this afternoon. She retrieves the postcard with a picture of Lookout Mountain and hands it to me. "Why don't you read it, Lexi?"

I turn the postcard over and begin reading. "'*July 20, 1959. Dear Mama, I just want you to know I'm alive. Sorry it's been two years and this is my first postcard. I've finally found her. I have done what I can to see her, but that's all I want to tell you about it. I've married a man from a lumber yard named Curtis Young. I hope you never meet him. You'd be happy to know I kept the last name James, just like you always wanted. But I didn't do it for you. Don't come looking for me, and don't try to help me. I love and hate you always, Lisa.*'"

I gaze at the letter and then at Mama, as dread grips my insides.

"Whoever she found must be the girl in this picture," says Daddy.

"I think so," says Mama, focusing on the second postcard, which she inches in front of Daddy and motions for him to read.

He clears his throat and begins. "*August 25, 1959. Dear Lisa, I'm glad you're not dead in a ditch somewhere. It would be best if you came back to Sleepy Oak. I don't want a life of struggle for you—a life that mirrors mine. Nothing waits for you where she is but heartache and disillusionment. I need my daughter now. I need your strength. Don't reject me for what I have done. You are the only one who can understand why I did it. Please come home. I love you always, Mama.*"

Daddy swings his gaze from Mama to me. We sit in silence for several moments, digesting the letters, no longer interested in the Chinese food growing lukewarm on our plates.

"What does the letter say?" asks Daddy.

Mama sighs and reads it with an unsteady voice. "*January 20, 1984. Dear Cindy, I've wanted to call you, but I'm afraid to tell you it's cancer. You've been gone for several years now, and even after all this time, I still can't figure out how to say I'm sorry for everything that's happened. We've had a hard life, and I'm guessing what you've just found inside the chessboard might make it even harder for you, but you're a James woman, so you need to know, just like I needed to know. It's in our blood, after all.*

"'*There's something waiting for you, exactly where I buried it, a few feet beneath the entry way of the crawl space of our old house in Chattanooga. You need to find a way to recover it and use it. Hopefully, your daddy is dead by the time you go looking for it. What you find will give you the answers you've wanted for so long, and it's the only way you can find her and save her in ways that I couldn't. You will know who she is soon enough. I love you, and I will always be proud of you. Love, Mama.*'"

Mama brushes away tears as her voice falls silent. A powerful presence hovers in the room. Clenching her jaw, she speaks with unexpected strength.

"We need to go there."

Daddy seems mystified. "You can't be serious?"

She nods. "Dead serious."

He shakes his head. "I don't think that's a good idea. It will be like digging up another dose of trauma for you. Besides, the girl in the picture could be dead or could have moved away from Chattanooga, if she was even there in the first place."

The fire swells in Mama's gaze. "But we *need* to know."

Daddy folds his arms and glares at her. "Why?"

"Because my mama wanted me to find her, whoever she is. It's important to have closure and find the answers I've craved my whole life."

Daddy's voice comes out strained. "Cindy, you've already found closure. Doing this will only make you form an unhealthy obsession again."

Mama's cheeks redden. "Lexi, maybe you should go to your room so your daddy and I can talk about this privately."

"It's okay, Mama," I say, placing my hand on hers. "I'm in this with you. I need to know too."

She stares at me, and I realize that she has feared this moment for years. Her expression acknowledges my awareness of the common poison that threatens us. These postcards and the letter have only reinforced the dark and twisted thoughts which have been lurking in my mind. Mama recognizes my struggle, the grappling to resist the same compulsions that once consumed her. I look at her, explaining without words that she can't shield me from the family curse because I am already living it. The horrific imaginings, the nightmares, the visions—it is in my blood and it is in my brain. Our only hope to end it is to find its source and face it together.

Mama shifts her focus to Daddy, transitioning into persuasion-mode. "We have to do this, Tony. What we find could change everything we know about my family. We've already let our CBT patients know that we're on hiatus for the summer, and Lexi is out of school now, so this is our only opportunity."

He grunts and shifts on his chair. "I'm not comfortable with this."

She leans toward him, emboldened. "We need you right now. I need you to care about this, the way you cared before."

It is quiet for a few moments. Then Daddy says, "I'm worried."

Mama sighs. "You're worried I'll revert to how I was?"

He avoids her gaze. "Yes. We've made so much progress, and you've been healthy for almost nineteen years. I don't think we can afford to jeopardize that."

More silence. Then Mama says, "We're going, and that's all there is to it. Please, trust me, Tony."

He winces. "This is a bad idea, and you know it."

Mama bulldozes his comment. "We're leaving later this week, after I get over this cold."

A painful silence ping-pongs between them.

Daddy stares at her. "Fine. We can go. I just don't understand the obsession."

With tears rising, Mama glances at me. "You understand, don't you?"

I nod. "Yes, Mama, I understand. More than I want to."

Cindy James

Three days later, we roll along the highway surrounded by darkness. The tall streetlights positioned along the road appear like giant fireflies glowing for a moment before passing out of sight behind us. Tony, having completed his driving shift an hour ago from Little Rock to Memphis, lies napping in the passenger seat, snoring with his mouth open. A green sign whizzes by on the roadside—reading *Nashville 66*. The rhythmic hum of the tires on the pavement fills my ears. I focus on the road, but my mind lies caught in a web of remembrance.

My memory takes me back to a hospital room. My sweaty hair mats to my forehead. The bed feels warm beneath me, the sheets tossed in disarray. Snuggled together, Tony and I cradle the swaddled bundle melting our hearts with precious yawns, feeble arm stretches, and bewildered blinks. Tiny fingers brush my hand, searching, fumbling, and then latching on in pure dependency. I take in her scent, the smell of perfect innocence. My lips smother her smooth forehead.

"You sure?" asks Tony.

"Yes, I'm sure," I say. "I want her full name to be Alexis. But to me, she's Lexi."

My memory moves me forward until I see Lexi's four-year-old figure scampering around the kitchen, caked in white powder. Standing at the island, I measure another cup of sugar and add it to the cookie mix.

"Mama, look!" yells Lexi.

I give her my full attention, watching as her flour-covered hands smear her grinning face.

"I'm a ghost, Mama! I'm a ghost! Ooo…"

She extends her arms and walks toward me with all the suspense she can muster. Laughing, I place my measuring cup on the counter and reach down to scoop her up.

"You're the prettiest ghost I've ever seen, Lexi!"

She beams with pride. "You wanna be a ghost too, Mama?"

I nuzzle her forehead with mine. "Of course, baby. As long as I get to be with you, I'll be anything you want."

"Can I get some more ghost powder?"

"Absolutely."

I pry one hand free, tip over the flour bag, and allow a handful to pour into my palm. Lexi cups her hands into a bowl and lets me deposit the magic face paint.

"Ready, Mama?"

"One," I say.

"Two," she replies.

"Three," we call in unison.

She catapults her hands onto my face, coating me with powder. She hops out of my arms and giggles erupt as we become ghosts haunting the kitchen. I chase her around the island until we collapse to the floor, laughing so hard that tears roll down my cheeks, streaking my flour mask.

The wonderful scene from the kitchen disappears.

My memory twists slowly into a nightmare, conjuring the image of a little blonde-haired girl sitting alone in a graveyard, her tiny arms reaching for someone to rescue her. She opens her mouth to scream, but I cannot hear her voice. The girl vanishes into the night air, leaving a wretched, bloodied man in her place—the embodiment of my childhood horror—grasping, cursing, straining to drag me and Mama back into the house of punishment. The resurfacing nightmare that never ends—Daddy.

A disorienting flurry of images comes next: a headless Raggedy Ann doll, a mansion, a red room, a fire, a new home, a husband, a daughter, a chessboard.

The memory web untangles, returning me to the car, leaving me gasping for breath. My hands clamp the steering wheel. Two ancient voices echo in my mind.

Cindy, what if there is a new series of memories waiting to be discovered, remembrances that will awaken the illness in you? How can you afford to take that risk?

But, Cindy, what you don't yet know about your family is what has kept you from feeling complete all these years. You know there are answers if you keep digging. How can you afford not to take that risk?

A beautiful eighteen-year-old girl stretching her arms and yawning in the backseat breaks my trance.

"You okay, Mama?"

I give her a weak smile. "I'm fine, baby. You can go back to sleep."

She slips a hand onto my shoulder, hoping the gesture will relax me. She can always tell when I am tense. My body remains stiff, coiled like a spring about to snap.

"I'm glad we're on this trip," she says.

I nod. "Me too."

She withdraws her hand. Silence looms for several moments.

"Maybe this will help us become normal," she says.

I concentrate on her reflection in the rearview mirror. "What do you mean?"

She pulls at her eyebrow with her fingers. "How we are—you know, the two of us—it's not normal, I think. I always thought you were happy, but you've been struggling, just like me, right?"

"I've been happy, Lexi," I say. My words sound forced.

She places her hands in her lap. She uses one fingernail to slice at her other nails. "I think maybe you've been hiding, Mama. I wish you would have told me before about your past."

I sigh. "I didn't want to scare you."

She blinks away tears. "But I've been scared anyway. I can't stop rubbing my wrists together, and tearing at my eyebrows, and slicing my fingernails. I have dark thoughts, and nightmares, and I see things."

My insides ache. "Like what, honey? What do you see?"

She looks out the window. "Images of myself dying. Visions of all of us dying. I see ghostly women surrounding a gravestone. I'm sorry, Mama. It's gotten worse this past year. I feel like I need to know how it started in the family, so I can know how to stop it."

"I'm sorry, Lexi. I know it's hard. You will have to fight against the sickness, just like I did. While you were growing up, I hoped we could avoid it by being positive and never focusing on thoughts that were dark or difficult, but I realize now that you will have the same conflict that I did. That's why this trip is so important. We have to make the cycle stop in our family. Just remember, you'll always have a choice, either to give in to those self-destructive thoughts or to resist them and fight for wholeness in yourself."

I stare at her intently, trying to tell her how sorry I am for placing her in this situation, for bringing her into a bloodline running with a toxic current of "crazy." She appears to understand my look and lets me know without words that it's all right. She wants to be here with me to face the darkness together.

"Why don't you go back to sleep?" I say. "You'll need your rest."

I watch her curl up on the backseat and drift into dreams again.

When we reach the motel an hour later, I nudge her, smooth her hair out of her face, and kiss her forehead.

Lexi James

The red Ford Taurus crests a hill and majestic Lookout Mountain comes into view. Daddy is driving again with Mama riding in the passenger seat. With her concentration set toward the mountain, she is lost in a fog of memories. We stare in silence as the road curves around the massive peak. Jagged rock formations, crags overlooking a frightening descent, and the expansive canopy of trees form a breathtaking sight. Even when the mountain passes out of sight behind us, Mama's focus remains fixed ahead. She seems engulfed in private pain, as if she cannot believe she is returning to this place almost four decades after she escaped from it.

Mama's bright pink T-shirt provides a stark contrast to her sullen mood. Dad wears his favorite attire: a red flannel shirt and faded, fraying blue jeans. I decided to go casual as well with a red University of Arkansas shirt and navy blue Capri pants. We're definitely dressed appropriately for digging up whatever Grandma Lisa buried for us to find. I just hope we'll blend in and not appear like outsiders in this city.

A few minutes later, Daddy slows the car and we cruise into the heart of downtown Chattanooga with its glimmering glass buildings and sprawling industry. Because of the congested traffic, Daddy takes an exit to the nearest gas station to give Mama a break. He shoots me a concerned glance in the rearview mirror. Neither of us wants to see her have a breakdown now. It would be terrifying for me, and a depressing reminder of history repeating itself for him.

"Why don't we stop for gas and then go eat," says Daddy, placing his hand on Mama's shoulder.

She nods in a detached manner.

"Good idea," I say, trying to keep my tone positive.

The moment we arrive at the gas pump, Mama opens her door and leaves the car. Daddy swivels in his seat to face me.

"Are you okay?"

My gut feels twisted into a knot. "I think so. I've never seen her like this before."

He scratches his head. "It might get worse before it gets better, but she'll be all right. Somehow, I believe she knows what she's doing. But could you go inside and keep an eye on her while I fill up the tank?" He grins wryly. "They never let me follow her into the women's restroom."

As usual, he's able to make me smile. "Sure thing," I say.

I hurry into the convenience store and find Mama in the center aisle, staring at the packaged chocolates. She seems unaware of my presence, as she piles up the sugary treats, cradling them against her chest as if they were precious infants. The plastic wrappers crinkle in my ears. When one entire section of chocolates has disappeared from the rack, I step closer to her, holding up my hands with caution.

"Hi, Mama. What are you doing?" I hear the shakiness in my voice.

"Getting help," she whispers.

Her fingers crawl toward another chocolate wrapper on the shelf, but I place my hand onto hers.

"Maybe we don't need all these," I say. "We're going to eat lunch now anyway, right?"

The intensity of her gaze causes me to step back.

"Fine, you take them," she says.

She dumps the pile toward me, allowing the chocolate treats to crash against my stomach and scatter across the floor. I stare at her, baffled. As tears rise, she bites her lower lip.

"You're right," she says. "I guess we'd better eat lunch. And buy a shovel."

Without another word, she turns and walks out of the store, leaving me to clean up the mess.

***

The car rolls away from Sugar's Ribs, a downtown Chattanooga hot spot famous for their ribs, which Daddy located through an online search on his cell phone. I can still smell the savory BBQ scent which permeated the atmosphere of the restaurant. The delicious BBQ ribs rumble in my stomach as we move toward the address Mama alone knows. While no one dares to speak, the mood hangs tense and expectant. All the while, my thoughts play a fierce tennis match, serving dread and returning panic.

Lexi Hexy, look at Mama. You're going to end up just like her—dazed, disturbed, and deranged.

Shut up, Alexis. You're always thinking the worst. Mama's fine. And I'm fine.

You've never believed that. Daddy doesn't believe that either. Watch him. Even now, he's trying to hide his fear, the fear that her sanity will snap like a twig again. He knows you're next in line for the family fallout.

With a lump in my throat, I view Daddy in the rearview mirror. He appears as if he has lost something. Now I realize why he didn't want us to come on this trip—it could change Mama, making her revert back to her "old self." It might also change me for the worse, tipping me face-first into the madness of the James women.

See, Lexi Hexy, I told you he knows she's crazy. You're going to lose some screws too by the time this trip is over. Well, actually, don't think of it as a trip—it's more like a freefall into "crazy." Pitiful thing. You never even stood a chance.

Alexis, get away from me. Mama's NOT crazy. She's just hurting.

Hurting? Is that the best you can do? How do you explain her being normal for as long as you've known her, but now she's foggy in the eyes and batty in the brain?

She IS normal. She's my Mama. I love her.

She's a nut job, and you've just helped her reopen the can of nuts. Good job.

Shut up!

Remember that scar on her wrist? She always told you it was a burn from cooking. Well, she lied. She cut herself. Attempted suicide! It only took her eighteen years—your whole lifetime—to fess up to you. She tried to slice and dice and bleed her way out of this life.

I don't want to talk about that.

You remember it, don't you? Don't you?

Yes, yes, I remember! She admitted it to me. But it's not going to happen again. We're going to find answers and get closure.

Sweet, stupid Lexi Hexy, you're riddled with the same curse. This searching will only stir up the nasty brew to infect you both further. Let it go. Leave. You don't need to know anymore. Stop interfering with the past.

No, we have no other choice but to finish it. We have to find out who we are in this family. Mama needs this. I need it.

Fine, but you know what's coming. Don't say I didn't warn you.

"How close are we?" Daddy's voice invades my ears.

I fidget in my seat. Then I realize he is talking to Mama, not me. She answers him with silence, still engrossed in her nightmare.

"Cindy, are you okay?" he asks, placing a hand on her knee.

"I want to do something before we go to the house," says Mama. "Turn left here onto Lookout High Street."

Daddy obeys and we cruise for a minute before reaching a one-level brick school building with a green roof. As we pull into the cul-de-sac near the front entrance, I notice the sign: *Lookout Valley Middle/High School*. Daddy parks the car and glances at Mama.

"Is this where you went to school?" he asks.

She swallows hard and nods. "Yes." Her expression is filled with sadness. "It seemed much bigger when I was thirteen."

Daddy smiles. "Things always seem bigger when you're younger."

"It's changed so much," says Mama. "Too much. I know it's been around forty years since I set foot in the school, but somehow I imagined it wouldn't be renovated or updated. I wanted it to match the picture I had in my head. Now I hardly recognize it."

"Is everything all right, Mama?" I ask.

She shakes her head. "Let's go. This is harder than I thought it would be. School is one of the only good memories I have of the city, and I want to remember the building the way it used to be in my mind, not the way I see it now. Can we leave?"

"Sure thing," says Daddy.

The car circles around the cul-de-sac and drives away from the school that Mama stepped out of for the last time on the day she and Grandma Lisa escaped and drove away to find a new future.

***

Several minutes later, we travel on a different road somewhere between Lookout Mountain and Mama's old school.

Mama has been navigating us, using the GPS function on her cell phone, choosing a direction, then changing her mind, and then changing her mind again. The road signs confuse me. I've seen I-24 E, US-27 N, Martin Luther King Blvd., Market St., Main St., and a slew of others. We've also encountered a series of landmarks: the Chattanooga Choo Choo, Walnut Street Bridge, The Hunter Museum of American Art, and the Tennessee Aquarium. It seems Mama is taking us on a deliberately roundabout tour of the city. Perhaps she hopes to visit every location in Chattanooga other than our intended destination. I remember my teacher once telling me a famous quote: "you can't go home again." At the time, I wasn't sure what it meant, but after seeing Mama's reaction to the city she once called home, I understand it now.

"Keep driving straight," says Mama.

After crossing a downtown intersection, I glimpse a bus stop sign, and I wonder if this is the same bus stop where Mama and Grandma Lisa stood when Grandpa Curtis' rusty red truck pulled up and he bellowed his threats to follow them if they left. I don't have the heart to ask Mama about it—she appears to be revisiting enough childhood trauma as it is. The bus stop fades out of sight, and we continue moving forward into her past.

Soon, we end up on a secluded stretch of road. We passed the last house several minutes ago. The roadsides sprawl with overgrown weeds. As the road curves, a small, dilapidated one-story white house comes into view on the left. It looks condemned, with the windows boarded up, spray paint art lining the walls, and broken glass lying about in the yard. The yard is nothing more than a patch of withered, brown grass.

Mama gasps, her entire body jolting in her seat. Daddy pulls the car into the dirt driveway close to the front door. He reaches up to rub her shoulder, as if attempting to work out a muscle knot. I glance from her pale, panicked face to the frail house—both appear ready to collapse at any moment.

Mama rummages in her purse and retrieves the letter which was hidden in the chessboard. After struggling to hold the paper steadily, she hands it to me.

"Are you all right to do this, Cindy?" asks Daddy. When Mama doesn't respond, he turns to glance at me. "Where does the letter say we're supposed to look?"

I scan the letter and read aloud. *"'There's something waiting for you, exactly where I buried it, a few feet beneath the entry way of the crawl space of our old house in Chattanooga.'"*

Daddy smiles grimly. "Are we ready?"

I nod and place the letter on the seat beside me. Mama doesn't acknowledge Daddy's question. Instead, she opens her door and steps out as if in a trance. We scramble out of the car to follow her. My heartbeat quickens as I reach her side.

"Mama, are you okay?" I ask, tugging at her sleeve.

She ignores me and moves toward the house. I follow her steps and take in the view. The outer walls are stripped and eroding, and the roof shingles have been pried off and are lying sideways in the storm gutter. The front door is sealed with a large sheet of plywood. Mama stares at the door and runs her fingers along its surface, as if trying to connect with a child who hides inside the house, afraid to come out from beneath her bed. Her hand trembles on the wood. She remains fixed in that position for almost a minute, while Daddy and I wait behind her.

Then, as if being snapped back to reality by a hypnotist, she jerks her hand away from the door and walks around to the back of the house.

"I guess this is my cue to get the shovel," Daddy mutters to me.

I nod to him and scamper after her. I hear glass crunching beneath my feet, followed by the sound of the car trunk opening and closing, as I arrive at Mama's side. We find a crawl space door at the base of the wall. Footsteps echo behind us, and Daddy appears, shovel in hand.

"I'll do the honors," he says.

He uses the shovel blade to break the rusty latch and nudge open the creaking wooden door. A whiff of musty air exits the black hole. Daddy turns his head away in disgust.

"Probably some dead critters down here," he says. "I don't suppose they make deodorant for crawl spaces?"

"I don't think so, Daddy," I say, half-smiling, thankful he is here to help lighten the mood.

Mama finds no humor in our dialogue. Her expression is intense, still absorbed by memory.

Daddy plunges the shovel blade into the dirt just beyond the mouth of the hole. With several dig-and-fling motions, Daddy progresses down two feet. He widens his carving area to include the crawl space entrance, ensuring he will find whatever is hidden. Sweat drips from his neck and forehead as he continues the excavation.

At the three feet depth, the shovel blade dings, striking something solid. He scrapes dirt from around the edges of the semi-buried object.

"What is it?" I ask.

"We'll see," he says, flashing his trademark grin.

Mama, who has seemed paralyzed for the past several minutes, now flinches. Her breathing becomes rapid, and her body leans forward with anticipation. After setting the shovel aside, Daddy reaches into the earth and pulls out a wooden box measuring a foot square. A sturdy lock secures the lid. Excitement floods my senses.

"Now we know what the key is for," I say.

Mama reaches into her pocket, retrieves the silver key, and hands it to Daddy, who inserts it into the lock. A turn, a click, and the box opens, revealing something wrapped in a garbage bag. Daddy opens the bag and retrieves a black leather book. We experience a reverent moment, as we stare at the artifact in awe. Daddy extends the book to Mama. At first, she appears overcome, leaning away from it, but then she grazes her fingers along its surface, as if communicating with it. At last, she takes the book from Daddy's hands and holds it to herself. She finally opens the ancient cover and begins reading, her eyes misting with tears.

"What does it say?" asks Daddy.

Mama continues reading to herself, as if we are no longer on the same planet.

"Mama?" I ask.

A flicker of awareness flashes in her countenance, yet she does not respond.

"Read it out loud, Mama," I persist.

She offers a deep sigh.

"Mama, please," I say, touching her arm.

When she speaks, shakiness reveals itself in her voice.

"'*April 10, 1957. I am writing this to myself to try to sort out the fog in my brain. I have never written a journal before, but lately I have felt compelled to start putting my story to page. Perhaps it might help silence the disorienting voices, calm the constant paranoia, and put to rest the endless nightmares. But how do I even begin? I have to give this painful poison a release onto something other than my sweet Lisa, so it might as well spill onto these pages. I hope she will never read this because she knows nothing of my history, and I hope she can find a way to forgive me for all the things of my life that I pray she never discovers. Elaine James.*"

Mama closes the journal, unable to read any further. We stand, waiting, unsure as to how to proceed from this point. The space between the three of us shimmers with tension. Then, without warning, Mama walks past us, around the house, and back to the car. Daddy and I share a quick, baffled glance and hurry to follow her.

PART TWO:

Sleepwalking

Cindy James

Lexi lies sleeping on the motel bed beside me, and Tony snores on the couch from the far side of the room. I, however, am wide awake. I glance at the alarm clock on the nightstand—4:30 a.m.—but I have not yet had a moment of rest. About an hour ago, Lexi was too emotionally exhausted to stay awake, and her body finally gave in to sleep. No wonder—we have been reading the journal for two days straight, unable to stop.

The howling wind echoes through the window pane. The motel walls creak and groan like those walls of the miserable mansion so long ago. Shadows streak the room, playing tricks on my mind. The black leather journal rests on the nightstand beside me, and a throbbing headache thunders through my temples.

I close my eyes and picture the three of us sitting on the edge of this bed hours earlier, reading the first page of Grandma Elaine's story. The words resonate within me as the page flowed in perfect cursive writing.

It is odd that I only remember when the bad memories began. As a result, the first five years of my life—the ones with Mama and Daddy—are wiped clean from my mind, erased as if they never happened. I suppose that's what is meant by a family curse: only having recollection of the nightmares, not the niceties, of your lifetime.

My first memory was from the summer of 1919, when I was six years old, and my twin sister, Julia, and I were standing by two large holes in the ground where Mama and Daddy had been placed to sleep forever. Men with shovels poured dirt onto their new box beds. We were never allowed to see the faces of Mama and Daddy during the funeral. The lids of the boxes were closed. A nice man with a briefcase walked around with us all day, encouraging us to say "goodbye" to the crying strangers.

My second memory was the nice man with the briefcase driving Julia and me to a town near a large lake. He called it Traverse City. That sunny day we arrived at a small house that smelled funny and looked like it might crumble into the ground. The front door groaned as it opened, and an old, scary woman stood waiting for us. The nice man opened his briefcase, handed her some papers and money, waved goodbye to us, and then hurried to his car and drove away. We never saw him again. The old woman curled her lip at us and told us to get inside the house.

My third memory was the lesson I learned that day, which I kept learning for the next twelve years—life is cruel.

As I drift off to sleep, my mind fills with someone else's memories. My thoughts are sleeping in Cindy yet awakening in Elaine, ready to relive her story in my slumber.

Elaine James

I walk hand in sweaty hand with my twin sister, Julia, into the creepy old lady's house. Julia has bright red hair tied up in pigtails, just like mine. My pink dress, identical to Julia's, feels dirty the moment we step inside. Something smells rotten in the house. The front door slams shut. We turn and see the yellow-toothed woman wearing a white robe which is torn at the edges and covered with brown and black stains. She towers above us, her nostrils flaring.

"What are you two uglies looking at?" she says.

I blink several times, trying to make the tears go away.

"Are we spending the night with you?" I ask, hoping she'll say "no."

The old lady laughs and stuffs the money and papers from the nice man with the briefcase into her pocket. "You'll be spending many nights with me. I need workers, and you need somewhere to stay."

Julia bites her lip. "Are Mama and Daddy coming to stay too?"

The woman scowls. "Your parents are dead. You went to their funeral, or don't you remember?"

Tears trickle down Julia's cheeks. I huddle close to her.

"Shh, Sissy, shh," I whisper.

The old woman marches into the dingy, cluttered kitchen, her feet thumping on the faded white tile floor. She places her hands on her hips. "My name is Aunt Verna. I'll let you call me that, I guess. Your mama was my sister. We weren't close. In fact, we hated each other. I didn't care for her, and she wanted nothing to do with me. It was better that way. I'm the closest thing you got to family." She turns and takes several large steps toward us, like an animal stalking prey. As she bends down to us, we can smell her hot breath. "But *we* sure as hell ain't family. I'm not gonna be your mama, and I definitely won't put up with no crying, needy girls in this house. Got it?"

Julia and I nod, without making a peep.

"Now, get out of my sight. You're already on my last nerve and you just got here. Your room is the last one on the left down the hallway. Go in there and go to sleep. I don't want no fussin'. I got paid good money for you two brats, so don't even think of running away. We're out in the middle of nowhere. If you ever set foot outside this house, wolves will tear the meat right off your tiny little bones, understood? You will eat, you will sleep, and you will work. If you're good, I'll let you learn how to read and write. If not, then I'll whip you. What are you waiting for? Get out of my sight."

I squirm and cross my legs. "Can I go pee, Aunt Verna, and can we have something to eat?"

Her expression grows dark. "What do you think this is, a hotel? Get out of my sight!"

She raises her hand and we scatter like cockroaches down the dark hallway to the last door on the left. As we enter our room, my whole body shakes with fear. I look at Julia's pale features, and I realize that the nice man with the briefcase has dropped us off in hell, and we won't be leaving anytime soon.

***

As I crouch beside Julia on the filthy basement floor, our bare feet wallow in soap suds while we scrub the same impossible red stain for the third time this week. The smells of old soap, sticky brown grime on the floor and ceiling, and black mold on the walls cause me to cringe. Rats scurry around us, nipping at our toes on their search for food. The pitter-patter of their tiny feet and their terrible squeaks fill my ears.

Our matching gray pajamas, which Aunt Verna made us sew, are nearly black with smears and smudges. I glance over at Julia, whose face mirrors mine. It is pale, sunken, streaked with dirt, and red-cheeked from contact with an open hand. Her unbrushed, curly red hair straggles across her scalp, no longer tied up in pigtails. Those bright blue eyes have a cloudy storm rising in them. She winces, as I do, at the touch of the cold floor beneath us, as frigid as the snow on the ground outside.

We share a mutual teary-eyed expression. No sooner has the knowing glance passed between us than the basement door swings open, and Aunt Verna stands with her hands on her hips and a sneer rising on her lips. I recognize her familiar unkempt gray hair, bony frame, and pock-marked cheeks. I also see her disfigured hands with fingers bent at unnatural angles, and my stomach lurches as I try not to stare at the hideous appendages.

She notices my terrified reaction. "What are you staring at, ugly girl?" Her raspy tone grates against my ears like nails on a chalkboard.

I concentrate on the soapy floor below my pruny hands.

"Look at me!" she hollers.

I obey, focusing on her hideous smile of crooked, yellow teeth.

She chuckles. "I know what you both deserve today, you ungrateful wretches—another four hours of work. Just because it's your birthday doesn't mean eighteen-year-old girls don't deserve to work hard. So keep scrubbing, my uglies."

She slams the door, and we face another four hours of labor.

***

Later that night, I sit at the crude brown table in the center of the run-down kitchen. A single candle on the kitchen counter illuminates the dining area. Aunt Verna sits at the head of the table, chewing loudly, smacking her lips, and wiping dribble from her mouth every few bites. Shadows creep across her face from the flickering candle. She glowers at Julia and me, scrunched side by side at the opposite end. The chair supporting the two of us groans with each movement. With trembling fingers, we shove stale bread into our mouths and scoop peas from one plate onto our spoons.

I see Julia blinking away tears. I raise my hand and wait until the old woman acknowledges my gesture, not daring to speak without permission.

"What do you want, ugly girl?" she says.

"Aunt Verna, may I use the bathroom?"

"No. Finish eating. You need strength to work."

I fidget with discomfort, causing the chair to squeak. "Please, Aunt Verna? I really have to go. I won't be trouble, I promise—"

Her gnarled hand strikes the table. "Shut your mouth, you worthless whiner."

We eat in tense silence for several moments. Then, against my better judgment, I raise my hand again.

"What now?" The biting quality in her voice sears like hot coals.

"I'm begging you, Aunt Verna. I think I might pee on the chair if I don't get to the bathroom."

"Then piss on yourself and sit in it, ugly girl. I don't care."

I squirm on the seat, nearly knocking Julia off. "Please!"

"Don't you get out of that chair, or you'll regret it," says Aunt Verna.

I hold myself still. My insides ache, twisted in liquid knots. I mutter something under my breath.

Aunt Verna's fork clangs on her plate. "What did you say?"

"Nothing," I say, swallowing hard.

"What did you *say*? I won't ask you again."

A shaky breath escapes my lips. "I said Mama and Daddy would have let me go to the bathroom."

I expect her to leap up from the table and approach me with fists swinging, but she remains seated, taking in my words. Then a belittling smile appears on her crumb-caked mouth. "But your folks are gone, aren't they? And so are your bathroom privileges for the rest of the night. I know you wish your parents were alive. So do I. Then I wouldn't have to deal with you. But neither of us is so lucky."

She waits for a reaction from me, but I give her nothing. After a moment, she grins. "Do you even know how your parents died? I bet the man who dropped you off here never told you, eh?"

Julia and I glance at each other in confusion. Aunt Verna cackles.

"I'll take that as a 'no,'" she says. "Well, I think it's a good night for story time. Consider it my birthday present to you. Seems your mama went crazy without ever showing it. Apparently, one night while you were being babysat at the neighbor's house, your folks were supposed to have a nice meal together at home—a date. Except this wasn't an ordinary date. No, my uglies. Instead of making dinner for the date, your mama grabbed a knife and played butcher with your daddy. Then she decided to carve a sculpture out of herself. A murder suicide date, that's what it was. Ah, what a shame. Murder and suicide. That's what you got in your bloodline, little brats. You don't stand a chance of being normal."

Julia grips my hand below the table. Tears streak down her cheeks. I grit my teeth and wipe my own cheeks dry. Aunt Verna seems unfazed, scowling at our emotion.

"But I ain't gonna feel sorry for you," she says. "You think you have it so bad? You don't know anything about pain. After my daddy died of the fever, my mama yanked me out of school and had me work on the farm eighteen hours a day. She was a cold-hearted, mean old wench. When I misbehaved—even when I behaved—she pounded on me. I got so bruised, I couldn't see straight or walk for days sometimes. I wanted to die each night, so I wouldn't have to see the next morning. Compared to what I got, you uglies got it easy. Sure, your parents died, but I take it easy on you with the labor. When I was your age, I worked on that farm, all day, every day, even in winter. I lost a couple toes to frostbite, but that didn't stop the whippings I got. I used to be weak like you. I used to whine, saying I deserved better. But whenever I complained, my mama didn't coddle me. No, she broke one of my fingers. That's how I got these."

Aunt Verna extends her gnarled hands toward us. My stomach turns. She notices my repulsion and sneers.

"You're disgusted by me, eh? You think you're so much prettier and better than me, don't you? Well, maybe I should give your fingers a break or two. Then we'll see if you think you're so beautiful. I have no sympathy for you two uglies because no one had sympathy for me. Life is cruel. Get used to it. You either toughen up and survive, or you wither and die. You uglies ain't worth my time. I never wanted you, and you haven't been worth the money they convinced me to take to let you mooch off me for life. You haven't earned the right to think you deserve anything better than what you've got in life, and you definitely haven't earned the right to use the toilet tonight with your disobedience. So, when I say no, what do I mean?"

I lower my gaze to the peas on my plate, finding them too small to hide behind. "You mean *no*, Aunt Verna." I wipe away tears.

"Well done, ugly girl. You finally got an answer right. Now finish eating. You should be glad I give you anything to eat at all. I'd be smarter to sell the two of you to one of the plantations. At least I'd get my money's worth then. Just for your smart-mouthing, you get two extra hours of cleaning the red stain on the basement floor."

Hate boils in my belly, but I keep my eyes down. I want to scream at her and tell her that the stain will never come clean, no matter how many nails we break, fingers we blister, or palms we shred trying to scrub it away. But I know she already knows that, and that's the reason she forces us to work at it.

"Yes, Aunt Verna," I say.

She grunts. "That's right, you better say 'yes' to me. Every day, I have to live with the regret of having you two dropped on my doorstep, disrupting my peaceful life. You're always complaining, always needing something. As if I'm some rich widow who has money to throw around to beggars like you. Now, shut up and finish your food."

Julia and I resume our silent pea-eating, not sure whether we have to partake of the second item on the menu tonight—chicken gizzards—which appear raw, slimy, and grisly and smell even worse. My stomach flips at the sight of them. Without thinking, I frown at their unwanted presence on the plate.

Suddenly, Aunt Verna flings her fork across the table in our direction. The pointed prongs turn over and over before bouncing off my shoulder. I wince at the pain, trying to hold back tears and struggling not to react.

"What did you say about me?" she bellows.

My face blanches. "We didn't say anything, Aunt Verna. We were quiet and finishing our food, just like you told us to."

Her expression contorts with rage. "I heard you mutter something about me under your breath. Think I'm too old and deaf to understand you, eh? Get out of my sight, filthy things. No reading, no talking, no nothing, except bed for both of you. Get gone, before I smack you raw."

She raises her right hand and we flee the kitchen. Swinging open the green paint-peeling door to our room, we crawl into our "bed," which is nothing more than a single thin blanket wadded on the hardwood floor. There is no furniture in the room. The only other items in the room besides us and our blanket are piles of rat droppings and thick, gray dust bunnies. The sound of clattering dishes comes from the kitchen, followed by Aunt Verna stomping down the hallway to lock our bedroom door from the outside so we cannot escape.

Julia and I lie pressed against each other, trying to keep warm under the blanket. Neither of us dares to speak, terrified that Aunt Verna is perched outside our door, listening for the slightest sound to give her a reason to barge in and give us more bruises. As I lay motionless, my bladder begins stinging again, needing release. I try to hold it, cringing as the pain shoots through my abdomen, but, after a few minutes, I end up crying into the crook of my elbow as urine runs down my legs. Julia strokes my hair and cries with me. We can't bring ourselves to speak about the horror of how Mama and Daddy died. The pain of it is too deep for words. We cry until we exhaust ourselves.

The warm wetness soon soaks through my pajamas. It turns cold and makes me shiver. I pray for sleep to rescue me from this nightmare. After two more hours, I escape at last from hell and vacation in dreams of a tropical beach where they celebrate birthdays for eighteen-year-old girls with cake, not cruelty.

***

I curl up with the blanket, still shivering, later in the night. The dark air keeps us pinned down like a bully. Julia lies cushioned against me on the stiff floor. Our bedroom remains quiet, except for the sounds of insects scratching nearby and the rats tunneling through the baseboards of the walls. Faint traces of moonlight peek through the barred bedroom window.

As if rising like a ghost from my own body, my mind travels from the bedroom to the hallway. I picture the black scuff marks on the once-white, now yellowish walls, evidence of Aunt Verna giving Julia or me a friendly slap, followed by a shove against the wall for missing a spot while polishing the cracked china dishes in the dilapidated living room hutch. It is equal opportunity punishment in Aunt Verna's house. She shows no favoritism—the only thing she is fair about. My mind glimpses Aunt Verna's bedroom door, but we don't dare enter. Instead, my imagining takes me to the living room and the pile of tattered books we are permitted to read on rare occasions. Books are our only form of socialization, the only interaction we can have with other people, even if the people are made-up characters. Apparently, the stack of books is some sort of consolation prize for not being allowed to go to school.

The most enraging part of living here, besides the abuse, is that we are forced to keep up a house that is falling apart. It is not a refined mansion or well-kept dwelling place. It is a rats' nest, and Julia and I are the rats. My mind moves me to the front door, which is always locked, and the smudged kitchen windows, which are barred. Aunt Verna's home is far from anyone, and Julia and I have never set foot outside for the past twelve years. Apparently, there are deadly wolves outside, waiting to tear us to pieces if we try to escape. I bet the wolves out there are not as vicious as the wolf in this house. Finally, my mind sweeps past the kitchen and returns to our bedroom, finding nothing of interest or hope elsewhere.

Julia shudders next to me, her whole body rigid from the cold that pierces through the paper-thin blanket. She sniffles, dabs tears, and blows onto her cupped hands.

"I—can't—feel my fingers, Lainey," she whispers.

"I can't either," I say. "Sissy, just close your eyes and try to think of a warm place, like a tropical beach."

She sighs. "We'll never get to see a place like that, so it's hard to imagine."

I kiss her forehead. "I know, Sissy, I know. That's why we have to dream about it. It can be real in our dreams."

"I'm so tired," she says. "I think I'm getting sick again."

I shake my head. "You can't get sick again. You know what she'll do."

She starts to cry. "I'm sorry, I can't help it."

"But she'll stop feeding you until you stop being sick. Just like last time. She'll punish you for getting sick and not being able to work as hard. You need food to keep your strength, Sissy. We can't survive another winter if you don't eat."

"It's so cold," she says, her voice muffled as she buries her face in her hands. "My bruises ache, especially the ones on my back. The cold makes them hurt even more."

I stroke her hair and fight back my own tears. "Shh, Julia. It's okay. We'll be all right. Just try to sleep. I'll take you some place warm once we get out of here."

"But we'll *never* get out of here," she whimpers. "It's been twelve years, Lainey."

"We'll be free someday, you'll see," I say, trying to keep my voice low. "It's our birthday today, and eighteen-year-old girls should be allowed to dream, so we're going to dream and hope for something better. We'll find a home somewhere, where no one beats us, where we can eat when we're sick, and where we can get paid for working. I promise you, Julia, I'm going to find a way. We're not going to die here."

I close my eyes, unable to bear seeing her pitiful expression.

***

When I awaken, it is almost dawn, though still dark. Julia slumps against me, her face bluish and her lips chapped. I nudge her and she stirs.

"Is she awake yet?" she asks.

I shake my head. "I haven't seen or heard her. She shouldn't be up for another hour or two."

She glances at the door. "Then why are we getting up so early? We can't leave the room."

I smile and lower my voice. "We're going to escape."

She snaps to alertness, sits up, and stares at me with astonishment. "What? There's no way out. The window is barred and the door is locked."

I place a hand on her shoulder for assurance. "We deserve something better than this, Sissy. I have a plan. Come on."

"Now?" she asks.

"Yes, now," I say. "Unless you want to spend another day scrubbing the red stain on the basement floor, eating raw chicken gizzards, and getting beaten."

Throwing the blanket off and standing to her feet, Julia indicates her answer, so I lead her to the door.

"What's your plan, Lainey?" she whispers, her voice shaking with anxiety.

I grin and remove from my pajama pocket a thin wire that is bent and folded several times in snake-like fashion.

"I made a lock pick from her umbrella," I whisper. "I stole the umbrella last week when she wasn't looking, broke the wire out of it, and then put it back. You can't even tell the wire is missing."

She nods and points to the door. "Good thinking, Sissy. Now let's go before she wakes up."

I maneuver the wire into the crack between the door and the outer wall, pressing its tip against the thick bolt. After several jabbing efforts, the wire catches the edge of the metal. I pry the bolt loose until the mechanism gives way and the lock releases. I wrap my fingers around the knob and turn it, cringing as the familiar squeak erupts. Then I thrust the door open, remembering its hinges creak less with rapid motion.

Julia and I hold our breaths as we creep into the hallway on our tiptoes. We pass Aunt Verna's bedroom, the living room, and the kitchen. As we arrive at the front door, Julia tugs on my arm.

Her voice trembles. "Are you sure about this? If she finds us, she'll whip us raw."

"I can't stand another day trapped like this. Let's go!" I whisper.

She sees my determination and draws courage from it. "Okay."

I insert the wire into the lock on the front door, but it is more difficult than the bedroom lock. Sweat appears on my forehead as I wiggle the wire tip against the bolt, waiting for it to catch the metal edge. My stomach jumps into my throat. The wire slips out of my moist hands and falls to the floor.

Suddenly, a door down the hallway flings open and Aunt Verna's hideous figure, covered in her stained white robe, lurches into view. She grins with delight, and she carries a kerosene lantern that illuminates our cowering bodies.

"Trying to escape, my uglies?" she says with a snarl.

I quickly scan the kitchen for any kind of weapon, but I see none. She takes a few steps forward, relishing our fear. Her thumping feet sound like thunderclaps in my ears.

"For this, you're gonna get the belt every hour on the hour for the next week," she says.

Backing against the wall, Julia and I stretch out our arms in a defensive gesture.

"Please, we didn't mean it," says Julia.

Aunt Verna steps within arm's-reach and places the lantern on the nearest end table. Her fiendish grin is appalling in the flickering light. "Too late to apologize. Go get the belt, so I can give you what you deserve."

Julia moves forward to obey. Then, as if stepping outside of my own body, I see myself reach out to hold Julia in place while shaking my head at Aunt Verna.

"No," I say.

"What did you say to me?"

I grit my teeth. "I said *no*! You can't keep us here anymore. We're leaving. We can make it on our own."

She jabs a bony finger at me. "Go get the belt, ugly girl."

I swat away her icy hand as a chill spirals down my spine. Her yellow teeth grind, and the hand I swatted away returns to strike my cheek. My tears rise and my cheek stings. Her grotesque hand clutches my throat and pins me to the door. My body grows rigid, refusing to be submissive.

"You're gonna do as I say, or you're not gonna be able to walk," she growls.

I struggle to breathe but still manage to shake my head, staring at her all the while with hatred.

She looks at Julia. "*You*, go get the belt! Now!"

Julia grasps my arm in terror. The old woman's eyes swell with spite, remaining fixed on Julia.

"Or maybe *you* should be the one I punish first?"

Aunt Verna glares at me, making sure I realize what she is doing. Instantly, I relent, relaxing my body.

"No, I should be punished," I say, defeated. "Do as she says, Julia. Go get the belt so she can whip me."

Aunt Verna, appeased for the moment, loosens her grip on my neck. Julia hesitates, then circles around us, pries open the basement door, and descends the stairs to fetch the belt from the nail on the wall.

"I'm sorry, Aunt Verna," I say, keeping my gaze averted.

She releases my neck and smacks my other cheek, re-emphasizing her point. Tears flow down both my burning cheeks. Her voice lowers to a menacing whisper.

"I'm still going to punish her first. And you're going to watch the whole thing. That will be your punishment. I know this whole escape plan was your idea. I will break you yet. Or maybe I'll just start by breaking some of *her* fingers."

A wild fury ignites in my head. As Aunt Verna's hand rears back to smack me for a third time, my submissive-self snaps, giving way to an empowering rage. Charging at her, I knock her off balance. She careens backward and topples to the floor. When she regains her composure, she closes her fist, ready to strike.

Without hesitating, I reach toward the end table, seize the kerosene lantern, and fling it at her face. The hot glass explodes into shards, spreading blood and flames across her skin. She writhes and grabs at her burning flesh. The lantern plummets to the hardwood floor and rolls into the kitchen, coming to rest against a pile of cleaning rags next to the stove. Aunt Verna screams as she collapses forward. Her head strikes the edge of the end table with a sickening thud.

Suddenly, all sound ceases.

I stand paralyzed for several moments, as bile rises in my throat. I turn away to block out the grisly sight and spot an orange glow coming from the cleaning rags. The basement door opens, and Julia emerges with a belt in her hands.

"What was that scream?"

"She's dead," I say, my breath coming in erratic bursts.

Julia glances from the body of Aunt Verna to the fire in the kitchen. Before she can form a response, I hurry over to her, grip the sides of her head, and capture her attention.

"She's dead, Sissy. Now we have to run away. The house is going to burn down, and we're going to let it. We need to find a new home, understand?"

She nods with a numb expression. The flames spread quickly through the kitchen, generating an intense heat that begins to thaw my frozen toes. I turn back to the body near the front door. I crouch down and rummage through Aunt Verna's nightgown pocket to find the house key. Unlocking the front door, I grab Julia's hand, and we flee into the morning darkness as the snow crunches beneath our bare feet.

***

My cheeks burn in the cold air as Julia and I cross the snow-encrusted street. It takes us nearly an hour of following the road before we find civilization. At the edge of town, a sign reads *Welcome to Traverse City, Michigan*. My gray, filthy pajamas are soaked through, and I have lost feeling from my feet to my shins. Once in town, we locate the public job listings board outside City Hall. Several people loiter around the board scanning the list, while their breaths escape in cloudy puffs. I lean in among the others, using my shoulder for leverage, and check for positions available for females. Huffing in frustration, I wrap my arm around Julia and lead her down the street.

"We need to find a place to stay for the night," I say, while I glance from one side of the crowded street to the other.

Julia shivers and paws at her reddened cheeks. "My throat feels like ice. I can't feel my feet."

I feign an air of confidence. "I know, Sissy. Don't worry. I'll find us somewhere to sleep."

"I'm scared," she says, wiping her nose.

"Me too. Let's get inside."

"But where? No one is going to take us in."

"There," I say, pointing to a quaint hotel nestled between two factories.

I lead her across the cobbled brick street to a two-story building, *Daydream Inn*. We enter through double glass doors into a small lobby area, with lounge chairs, end tables for books and newspapers, and a semi-circle front desk. The polished dark wooden furniture, the cream-colored walls, and the countryside pictures on the walls provide a welcoming environment. At the desk, sits a handsome man with a jovial, round face, who wears a brown corduroy suit jacket and looks to be close to our own age. His thick black hair sweeps sideways, his eyes shine, and his cheeks glow. He waves at us as if we are long-lost friends.

"Good afternoon, Ladies. Have you made a reservation?" His voice is strong and kind.

"No, I'm sorry, we didn't," I say.

Silence is his response, as he examines our haggard appearance.

After an awkward interval, he finally asks, "Are you all right? You look like you're freezing."

"It's very cold outside," whimpers Julia.

He smiles, his compassionate gaze rapt on Julia. "Yes, it's bitterly cold today. Definitely not any kind of weather to be out walking in."

"We'll be fine, thank you," I say, trying my best not to seem weak. "We just need some shelter for the night."

The man sorts through his desk, then he stands and circles around the desk within an arm's length of us. "You don't have any shoes! And where are your coats?"

Julia steps forward, almost touching him, her expression frantic. "We don't own any shoes or coats, sir. We don't have money. We don't have anything. Please, help us. We're desperate."

I tug at her arm, embarrassment rising in my cheeks. "Julia, please—"

Oddly, the man seems unflustered by her display of neediness. His understanding gaze is unexpected, but welcome.

"You are homeless?" he asks.

Julia nods.

I extend my hands in a defensive posture. "Sorry, sir, we don't mean any trouble. Perhaps coming here was a bad idea. Do you know of a women's shelter nearby where we could stay for the night?"

He sighs. "I'm sorry, but the nearest shelter is on the other side of the city. I'm afraid it will be a brutal walk for you."

I grasp Julia's arm and pull her toward me. "We understand, sir," I say. "We better start walking now while it's still daylight."

"Where are you going?" he asks. "Did I say you *couldn't* have a room?"

"What?" I stammer. "But we don't have any money. We've already told you that."

He raises his hand and places a key into Julia's trembling palm. "Room number twelve upstairs. Have a good day."

We stare at him, stunned.

"I don't understand, Mr.—" sputters Julia.

He grins. "Charles Newark. I own and manage this hotel. It's a pleasure to meet you. I hope you have a pleasant stay."

"But we won't be able to pay you," I say insistently.

He shrugs. "Why waste money that you don't have on renting a room here? You are my guests."

Julia struggles to hold back her tears. "This doesn't make any sense, Mr. Newark—"

"It's Charles," he says, giving her an affectionate glance.

She blushes. "Charles. Why are you doing this for us?"

His smile reassures us. "Because people helped my family when we needed it before, and I just want to do the same for you now. All meals are served through the double doors to your left. I will meet you there in an hour, and I'll be your host for breakfast today, if you don't mind. You will find clean towels in your bathroom and hot water in the shower. I'll send fresh clothes, shoes, and coats to your room as soon as possible, free of charge. If you need anything else, please don't hesitate to let me know."

Julia stares at the room key in her hand in disbelief. "Thank you—Charles—this is the nicest—the kindest—"

He waves her off and grins again. "Please, don't worry about it. I would only like one thing in return."

"What's that?" she asks.

"Please tell me your names. I always want to know the names of guests I invite to stay at my hotel."

"I'm Elaine James," I say, shaking his hand.

"Nice to meet you, Elaine," he says. His focus is magnetically drawn to my sister. "And you, Miss?"

"I'm Julia James."

"The pleasure is all mine," he says with unabashed charm as he cradles her hand.

Another blush floods her cheeks.

"Now," he says, "don't let me keep you from freshening up and relaxing from your difficult travels. I will see you soon."

He stretches his arm toward the stairs. After trading baffled expressions, Julia and I slowly climb the stairs to the second floor.

***

I survey Room 12, where we have been recovering for the past forty minutes. The walls are painted with soothing green and brown earth tones. Pleasant countryside scenes are depicted in pictures on the wall. A tall, dark wooden bookcase stands in the corner, filled with books of every color and size. Surely we have arrived in paradise.

After taking a scalding shower to revive her body, Julia crawled onto one of the queen-sized beds, covered herself with the thick comforter decorated with an evergreen tree pattern, and fell asleep. I waited until she was asleep before I showered, letting the hot water burn away my frozen state. Afterward, I sit on the edge of her bed, wrapped in a white towel, watching over Julia.

Finally, the tension in my body relaxes. For the first time I can remember, I don't smell like one of the rats from Aunt Verna's house. I rise from the bed, trudge back into the white-walled bathroom, and stare into the mirror. The eighteen-year-old girl gazing back at me seems twice her age. Fatigue, fear, and living a nightmare are impressed permanently on her features. This image concerns me. It also scares me. Who is this girl, and how has she become *me*?

Lainey, you're going to grow up to be unstable and broken. You don't have any strength in you.

No, Elaine. I'm not listening to you. I can make it through this. There's hope for me and Sissy. This kind man, Charles Newark, will help us. You see how he favors Julia. I will use that to our advantage, so I can save her and make sure she is secure.

Lainey, you're so naïve. Mr. Newark is just like Aunt Verna, only in a different disguise. Don't trust him, and don't fall for his fake generosity. He'll turn on both of you and abuse you. Life is cruel, remember? There's a curse in your blood. Your mama gutted your daddy and then did the same thing to herself. Your aunt was a vile woman. And you and Sissy are doomed to lose your minds to madness. You're already a murderer.

Get away from me, Elaine! You lie!

Don't fight the dark future. You're only fighting yourself.

My features in the mirror transform into Aunt Verna's, burning alive, the hideous image taking away my breath. I shudder, splash water onto my cheeks, and hurry from the bathroom without drying off. After collapsing onto the bed beside the sleeping Julia, I curl up and allow the tears to come. Emotional salty water crisscrosses my nose and cheeks, spreading out like a river in search of a calm sea.

While I wait for the breakfast appointment with our host, I weep over my lost life—the life that I was prevented from having. I'd always wanted a Mama and Daddy who were still living, a happy home where we could share laughter and memories, making friends in school, dreaming of going to college, and carefree years as a child where anything was possible. Instead, I had gotten bruises, slaps, and starvation, and, most painful of all, no hope that I would grow up to have a fulfilling life, or even a normal one.

***

An hour after first arriving at the *Daydream Inn*, Julia and I descend to the lobby, wearing the most expensive dresses we've ever seen—Julia's is ruby red and mine is sky blue—which were brought to our room by a bellhop, courtesy of our gracious host. We walk to the front desk where the kind, handsome Charles Newark waits. He stares at Julia.

"You look lovely, Ladies," he says.

Julia blushes. "Thank you."

"How are the accommodations?" he asks cheerily.

Julia smiles. "Wonderful. Thank you. We can't repay your generosity, Mr. Newark."

He chuckles. "I wouldn't expect you to. That's why it's generosity, not a loan. And remember, it's Charles, not Mr. Newark."

"Sorry—Charles," she says shyly.

He rises and gestures toward the double doors on the left. "This way, please."

We follow him into the dining room with its decorative earth tone wallpaper mix of greens and browns, just like Room 12. The homey place settings include simple green wreaths and beige candles in the center of the white tables. Several other guests are engrossed in lively chatter, laughter, and hearty breakfast portions. The scene is surreal in its innocent joy.

Within moments, Julia and I are led to a special table with a placard labeled RESERVED FOR MANAGER. Charles Newark eases out cushioned chairs and waits for us to take our seats. He sits across from us, beaming. Julia seems captivated by him, but I turn my gaze away, wondering if we made a mistake by joining him here. Surely we do not belong in such a pleasant place. I look around nervously, waiting for the guests to spot the ones who do not *fit*, whispering among themselves about "those girls," asking each other "what are *they* doing here?" But no one seems to notice us.

A gray-haired waiter, clad in a white apron, emerges from the kitchen and sweeps over to our table. The delicious scents of eggs, sizzling bacon, and hash browns waft into the room with him.

"Good morning, sir! What'll it be?" he asks, grinning. "The usual?"

Charles beams. "Hi, Louis. Make that three usuals, please. I'd like you to meet my new friends, Miss Julia James and Miss Elaine James." He gestures toward us.

The waiter waves his hand cordially. "I'm Louis, the chef," he says. "So nice to meet you both. I hate to brag, but prepare yourselves for the best breakfast you've ever tasted."

Julia and I grin. Satisfied, Chef Louis nods and flows back into the kitchen.

I watch Charles closely, as my thoughts continue to swirl. He offers a smile and then stares at Julia, enraptured.

"So, where do you intend to go from here?" he asks.

Julia and I trade wary glances, wondering how much we should admit.

"We don't know," I say, trying to keep my voice even. "We have to keep moving though."

"Really?" he says. "That's unfortunate." He scratches his forehead.

"It's just safer that way," I mutter, almost under my breath.

"I see," he says, raising an eyebrow. "Do you plan on walking the whole way to wherever you might go?"

"We have to," says Julia, averting her gaze.

"That sounds like nonsense to me," he says.

"I beg your pardon?" I ask, preparing to grab Julia's hand and bolt from the room.

He shrugs. "Well, I think it's foolish for anyone to walk the city roads downtown in weather like this, especially sweet, pleasant ladies like you. It's not safe to go out on your own."

I glance away, scratching my fingernails together. "We'll be fine, sir."

Julia breaks in with desperation. "We have no other choice, Charles."

I glance his way and find a look of compassion. He folds his hands on the table.

"I want to make you an offer, Julia and Elaine."

"An offer? What do you mean?" asks Julia.

"I would like for both of you to live here in this hotel for free, for as long as you'd like."

I can't hide my shock. I study his expression but find no traces of guile.

"I don't understand," I say. "There must be some sort of catch."

He shakes his head. "No catch. Just a promise of safety. You're obviously in a difficult situation, with nowhere to go and no one to turn to, so I want to give you a place to stay while you figure things out."

I do not blink for several moments.

"Why are you doing this?" asks Julia, bewildered.

He gazes out the window, as if re-entering a memory. "My father built this hotel from the ground up, and when he passed away three years ago, he left it to me to manage. He always emphasized treating people with dignity and respect, especially those who have fallen on hard times. The country has just gone through The Great Depression. Everyone needs help. Besides, I wouldn't be a gentleman if I let both of you walk out the front doors and back into danger."

"But you don't know anything about us," says Julia, her voice quavering.

He smiles. "What I've learned from the few minutes I've spent with you is enough."

"You're not curious about our past or what brought us here?" I ask, prepared to be on the defensive.

"No. You're here, and that's all that matters. So, what do you think about my proposal?"

"It's very generous, but how can we trust you?" I say.

A grin crosses his mouth. "You'll just *have* to trust me."

Julia leans toward him. "How can you trust *us*?"

His smile widens. "I'm not saying I trust you. I'm only saying that you now have an option other than wandering through the town and struggling to survive. If you stay here, you'll have all you need until you want to leave. No one should have to go through life alone."

My wrists would normally be rubbing together compulsively, but my hands continue to rest quietly on the tabletop. Julia glances at me with wonder. Before I can ask Charles to give us more time to discuss our decision, Julia reaches out and grasps his hand. She beams with a joy I have never seen before.

"We'll stay," she says.

***

Julia enters Room 12, radiant in her purple party dress, her cheeks flushed and her countenance dazzling. I am sitting at the desk, wearing a plain yellow dress not half as flattering as hers, reading *Jane Eyre* for the second time in as many months. Ever since Charles hired a tutor to help fill in the gaps of Julia's and my education, I have adopted a love of classic literature. Learning is one small way that Sissy and I are overcoming the inferiority complex that Aunt Verna instilled in us. As Julia floats into the room and leaps onto the bed like a carefree child, I lower my book and study her with suspicion.

"You're in a pleasant mood," I say, mustering a smile. A lovely scent drifts into my nose. "What is that smell?"

Julia smiles. "Perfume. Charles bought it for me."

"I've never smelled anything like it before. It's powerful."

"It's wonderful," she says.

I nod in agreement.

She releases a contented sigh. "I think I'm falling in love." Her voice is wispy like a breeze.

"Really? After three months? Don't you think that's a bit hasty?"

Julia seems surprised. "He's perfect. I can't find anything wrong with him."

I smirk at her. "That's because you've only known him for three months."

The vitality in her demeanor is endearing. She props herself on the edge of the bed, as if ready to tell an enchanting story.

"He took me to a fancy restaurant for lunch today. There were so many utensils next to the plate that I didn't even know what to do with them. We ate seafood shipped by his special order. Can you believe that? He had lobster sent in from the coast, just for me!" Redness colors her cheeks. "Yes, I think I'm falling in love."

I purse my lips. "With him or with the lobster?"

Julia giggles. "Nice try, Sissy. He's fantastic. Don't you like him?"

I shrug. "He's very generous and kind, but I would be careful about going head over heels for some rich man you've only known long enough to be impressed by. Right now, you only see him as fantastic, not flawed."

She huffs and twiddles her fingers. "You're just being overprotective."

I nod. "Always."

"So, have you been picking him apart to find a fatal flaw?"

"I've been keeping watch."

"And have you found anything yet?"

I sigh. "Honestly, I can't find anything. He seems genuine. A good man."

Julia beams. "I told you so. Now, will you let me fall in love already?"

I hold out my hands with emphasis. "Just promise me you'll be careful and not trust him with too much too soon."

A contagious smile ripples across her lips. "I'll trust him until he gives me a reason not to trust him."

I smile. "That's what I was afraid of."

***

Julia bursts into the room, this time fashioning a sublime light green evening gown, interrupting my reading of *Wuthering Heights*. With her face aglow and her steps lilting, she seems to float on a cloud. Her demeanor telegraphs the news.

"Lainey, I'm engaged!" she shouts, throwing herself into my arms.

I stand and fumble to catch her.

"Congratulations, Julia," I say. "I knew this was coming."

She pulls away to inspect my reaction. "And you approve, right?"

I smile. "Yes, I approve. You two are a perfect match."

A pang nags at my gut.

She is leaving you, and you will be alone, Lainey.

Julia breaks our embrace and paces the room. "We need to set a date, we need to choose a caterer, and we need to make a guest list." She stops and turns to me, as if suddenly remembering something important. "Will you be my maid of honor?"

"Of course, I will."

"Wonderful," she says. Then she resumes her pacing, lost in engagement bliss. "A jazz band will work well. We'll need to book the finest venue in town. Spare no expense, as Charles says. What else? I need to pick out my wedding dress. And then there's the reception dinner menu. So many things to plan!"

I reach out and grip her shoulders, holding her in place. "Calm down, Sissy. Everything will be fine. We'll work on everything together, okay?"

She takes a deep breath. "Okay. Thank you for being here with me. This is the most exciting day of my life, and I get to share it with you. You're the whole reason I'm here."

I kiss her forehead. "I won't let anything bad happen to you, Julia. I will always be here for you. Now, where is Charles?"

She places her hands on her cheeks. "I left him downstairs."

"You mean he proposed, you said 'yes,' and you just raced up here to tell me, leaving him alone?"

She giggles with embarrassment. "I guess I did. I'd better see if he still wants to marry me."

I pat her head. "Go find him. I'll be here reading."

Julia stomps her foot and smiles. "Are you kidding me? We're going to celebrate. Leave that book on the desk. You're coming with us. It's cocktail time."

She grabs my hand and pulls me toward the door. As we leave the room, one thought pulses through my brain.

She is leaving you, and you will be alone.

***

On a bright, summer day in 1932, the church is arrayed with pink and purple flowers, white ribbons, and a multitude of strangers. As I watch Julia and Charles at the altar, I have a joy I have been waiting for many years. A stunning white wedding gown complements Julia like a stabilizing garment, ensuring her future happiness. Charles, handsome as always, appears dapper in his black tuxedo. They recite their vows to each other, and I sense that my duty to watch over Julia is shifting to this honorable man. I am glad that he will be able to take care of her, but I am also saddened to relinquish my role as her protector.

Lainey, look at them. So happy. They fit together seamlessly. But where do you fit? Where is your place, where is your special someone to protect you? You have no one. You are alone now.

The minister announces them as man and wife and the crowd of strangers around me erupts in applause. Julia James has become Julia Newark—a new identity. She's only nineteen years old, and already the James in her is being blotted out, leaving me the only one to carry on the family name. The newlyweds smile, wave, and proceed down the aisle. As Julia passes me, she whispers, "I love you."

I reach to grasp her hand, but she is beyond my grasp as Charles pulls her to his side. A pain settles in my chest, an ache I cannot soothe. Julia and Charles exit through the double doors into the foyer, out of my sight.

Where do you fit, Lainey? You are alone now.

***

I glance around the grand living room, marveling at the spotless hardwood floor, stone fireplace, vaulted ceiling, and intricate crown moldings. Julia and Charles emerge from the next room, their footsteps echoing on the hardwood, followed by a man in a stiff black business suit.

"So, what do you think?" asks Julia, barely able to contain her excitement. "It's in the country, away from the city. Such beautiful scenery out here in the middle of nowhere. Do you like it?"

"It's incredible," I say. "This is the perfect place for you two."

Julia and Charles exchange glances and smile. Charles clears his throat, as if ready to make an important announcement.

"Elaine, we would be honored if you would live with us in this house," he says.

I scan their expressions, searching for signs of a joke, but they are sincere.

"What?" I stammer.

Julia nods. "I told Charles that I would only marry him if the house we owned had enough room for you to stay, too."

Charles grins. "I was already planning to have you live with us even before she asked me."

I am speechless, my mouth agape. In response, Julia rushes over and flings her arms around my neck.

"We wanted it to be a surprise," she says.

"I—I—I'm—"

Julia releases me and kisses my forehead. "Surprised?"

All I can do is grin.

Charles turns and shakes hands with the finely dressed realtor. "It's official. We'll take it."

The realtor's expression lights with dollar signs. "Excellent, Mr. Newark. I'll return to my office to begin the paperwork. I'll see you soon."

"Thank you," says Charles.

Julia slips her arm around my shoulders. "No more hotel living for us, Sissy. We're going to have a real home—just like we always dreamed."

Pointing to our left with a broad gesture, Charles says, "Elaine, you'll have that entire wing to yourself, with your own bedroom, bathroom, and library. I'll make sure to stock the library with books. All the classics, of course. Julia tells me you've always wanted that."

I blink away tears. "Yes, thank you. I'm overwhelmed."

He smiles. "You saved Julia and brought her into my life, so you're the one I should be thanking."

Julia gives me an affectionate squeeze. "I've never been happier in my life."

"Me neither," I reply.

I wait for the voice in my head to tell me otherwise, but it remains silent as we celebrate and begin making preparations to inhabit our new home.

***

Both light and darkness have lived with us in the house since we moved in eight years ago.

For the first three years, we shared laughter and happy moments as a normal family. Fishing trips, hiking jaunts to the forests, summer picnics in the park—we soaked up everything

Traverse City had to offer. The locale near Lake Michigan availed us of many nature activities and breath-taking sights. Sometimes I would read a book under a shady tree cover to cover in one afternoon. I came to know many of the town's local merchants by name, hearing their stories, supporting their businesses, joining their dinner parties, and sharing in their lives. The same town that had fostered so many bitter memories of my youth grew kinder with age, like dirty water slowly changing into fine wine. Our life in the house was simple and we cherished each other's company. Charles became like a brother to me. The two of us watched over Julia, ensuring her safety and happiness.

On New Year's Eve, 1935, just after the stroke of midnight at a noisy house party involving several of our tipsy friends, Julia announced to Charles that she wanted to have a child. We were ecstatic. Both Julia and I were twenty-two years old at the time. She later told me that she had always hoped to be a mother by the age of twenty-three. I asked her where she had come up with that idea, and she said she had had a dream on the night of our eighteenth birthday while lying on the cold bedroom floor at Aunt Verna's house. In her dream, she had delivered a perfect baby girl on her twenty-third birthday. When she woke up the next morning, she remembered the dream and promised to keep herself alive long enough so it could come true. I hugged her and told her I was thrilled for her.

However, our joy did not last long because we subsequently learned that Julia was barren.

Then darkness descended, casting gloom on the house. The laughter stopped. Julia was despondent for months, locking herself in her room and crying for hours. Charles and I tried to cheer her, but she sank further into depression.

My own depression soon followed. A deep, drowning sort of depression. I dreamed about knives, a collection of knives hidden everywhere, ready for use. When I lay in the bathtub, I pondered opening my veins with a blade and falling asleep forever in the red water. When I chewed food, I pictured it expanding in my throat like sharp steel, stabbing the breath out of me. I developed a fascination with death, a bizarre belief that dying was an appealing escape from pain, a way to avoid life's continuing disappointments. In some strange way, the reality that those I loved most would always be childless bereft me of my own hope for the future. Julia's barrenness was especially crippling because her fondest hope was lost, and without hope, it all seemed meaningless.

For the past five years since the sad news, we have lived our lives with an ever-present shadow of sadness lurking near. We have tried to make the best of things by never speaking about the situation. Life must go on, we decided, and so we've become experts in distracting ourselves with living. Our laughter has returned, but it is more subdued than before. We have continued to enjoy Traverse City, but the scenery has lost much of its allure. Charles has expanded the *Daydream Inn* and furthered his little empire, while Julia and I have busied ourselves with volunteering for local charities, as well as thriving in a home where birthdays are celebrated with cake instead of cruelty.

Yet, for all of our collective progress, there still seems to be a common emptiness among the three of us—a hole in the form of a baby.

***

May, 1940, has arrived and the sun teases us with hints of the hot summer to come. As usual, I am reading—*The Turn of the Screw*, this time—when Julia enters my library, wearing a long-sleeved gray shirt and dull, faded black pants, her cheeks streaked with tears. I can tell simply by the lack of color in her attire that something is wrong. I drop the book and rush to her side.

"What is it? What's wrong?" I ask, enfolding her in a hug.

"I have something to tell you," she whispers.

I lead her to the red loveseat, worried she might break into a thousand pieces at any moment.

"Tell me," I implore.

Her frown twists into a smile. "I'm pregnant. Surprise."

I gasp. "Are you serious? How did this happen?"

She nods and bites her lower lip. "It's a miracle. I'm so happy. I'm going to be a mother, and you're going to be an aunt. Can you believe it?"

I stare at her incredulously. "How is this even possible? You were barren."

Her countenance glows. "I don't know. We just never stopped trying. Somehow I believed that it might happen for us."

We share a bewildered smile.

"Pregnant," I say, almost to myself. "My Julia, pregnant."

Contentment flows over her. "I'm due in December, the doctor says. I might be having a Christmas baby. A little angel."

I take her hand. "I'm thrilled for you, Julia. I'm so glad you have the life you want."

The life you wish you had, Lainey, isn't that right? A little jealous, are we?

"Have you started picking out baby names yet?" I ask.

She glances away, as if the perfect baby's name floats somewhere in the room. "No, not yet. I hope it's a girl."

"I'm sure it will be. I just can't believe this."

"It really is a miracle," she says.

I stare at her in a daze. "This is amazing."

We sit, enjoying the silence for a moment. Then Julia stirs, engaging a new train of thought.

"So, any prospects for you, Sissy? Any dashing men that have caught your fancy?"

I laugh and avert my gaze. "Not a single one. All the men I meet are friends of Charles. I'm surprised you've let him try to play match-maker for me."

I glance back to Julia, who scrunches her forehead, deep in thought. "He knows some decent guys. We need to get you married. You need a man in your life."

I smirk. "So he can control me and run my life?"

Julia scowls. "That's not what Charles does with me, and you know it. Marriage isn't a power struggle."

I sigh. "It isn't for you because you married the right man. What if I'm not that lucky? How can you really know a person, know what they're thinking, know what they're capable of doing?"

"Are you all right, Elaine? I've never heard you talk about this in such a pessimistic way. I thought you *wanted* to get married."

I stand and move to the window, watching the tree branches sway in the breeze. Tears collect unbidden.

"I do. I just don't want to settle. I'm twenty-seven years old, Julia. I'd rather be alone than attached to the wrong person for life."

You're going to be alone anyway, Lainey. No one will want you once they know what's going on inside your head. Don't bring anyone else into this madness. Protect yourself, fight for yourself, and keep your distance.

Julia joins me by the window. "I think you're going to find the right man. You just need to keep your eyes open. You're the smartest person I know, Sissy. I'm sure you'll figure it out."

I continue observing the trees outside the window. "Congratulations on being pregnant, Julia. You're going to be a wonderful mother."

"So will you someday," she says.

We continue to talk, but all I hear in my mind is a voice of warning.

Keep your distance.

***

My wing of the house is quiet, just the way I prefer it nowadays.

Julia and Charles have gone into town on a shopping spree to celebrate their love and soon-coming baby, leaving me alone. I sorted through my closet earlier, seizing garments with bright colors and flinging them to the floor. I knew I needed something drab today, something to match my mood. An hour later, I emerged, wearing all black. For the past two hours, I have been wandering between my bedroom and the library, checking and double checking my precautionary measures. The atmosphere in my wing of the house feels like a fog, a suffocating force playing tricks with my mind.

The baby is almost here, Lainey. Soon you will be replaced. They will kick you out of their house. This is not your home. You are a guest whose time is running out. You don't fit anywhere, remember?

I sort through books on the shelves in the library, putting them in alphabetical order, then rearranging them randomly, and then replacing them alphabetically.

You are the outsider, the intruder, the eternal tag-along. They are perfect together and they have all they need in each other. You have nothing to offer. You are worthless to everyone you love.

I tear the sheets from my bed, then remake it, tucking in the corners, creasing the folds, fluffing the pillows again and again and again. Because there is too much dust, I must clean. I find the feather duster and set it to work on the nightstands, the lamps, the dresser, the headboard, and the baseboards.

No sane man will marry an insane woman. You are penniless and without prospects. Who will want to be with you?

When the dusting is done, I lock the door, then unlock it, then lock it, then unlock it. Still not safe. I must check the precautionary measures once more.

When they come to take you away—and they will—you need to protect yourself. This is why we hide them everywhere, remember? Make sure they have not been found.

I walk to one of the bookcases in the library. Pulling out the middle copy of my five copies of *Jane Eyre* reveals a knife. I replace the book. I move to the next bookcase, where I remove the middle copy of my five copies of *Wuthering Heights*. Knife, check. I do the same with *Frankenstein*, *Dracula*, and *The Turn of the Screw*. Three more books, three more knives. Excellent.

Check the others to make sure they are safe.

I hurry to my bedroom. Between the mattress and the box spring—knife, check. In each drawer of the two nightstands—check, check. Under the cushion of the armchair—check. In the dresser drawers—check, check, check, check.

I sit on the edge of the bed and breathe a sigh. All the precautionary measures are accounted for.

Good job, Lainey. When they come to take you away, you'll be ready.

***

Snow began to fall this afternoon, and it has continued all day. What started as tornado speed winds and heavy rain has swirled into a monstrous blizzard. The storm rakes the outer walls and piles the snow against the house in giant drifts. It is Monday, November 11, 1940, Armistice Day, a day to celebrate the end of World War I, but the snowstorm seems to foretell impending calamity.

Charles, Julia, and I have huddled together on the plush white couch in the spacious living room, listening to the house groan from the weight of the snow's accumulation. The angry wind howls, and Julia seems terrified, her hands trembling and her cheeks flushed. Charles has tried opening the front door but was unsuccessful. We are trapped inside, isolated. The nearest house is two miles away. The phone lines are dead. Charles lit a log fire, but it can only keep us warm for a little while. The pile of wood at the backside of the house is unreachable for now. We will have to wait out this storm.

Charles has wrapped himself in several layers, appearing rather laughable in his snow pants and enormous down coat. But no one is laughing. The atmosphere is thick with tension. I slip my favorite pink sweater on and then off every thirty minutes or so, indecisive about whether I should be warm or cold. Julia joins me in her fluctuating temperature. As the latest wave of shivers comes over her, I wrap her with a blanket, careful not to bump her bulging belly. She winces.

"What's wrong?" I ask.

She struggles to smile. "The baby is kicking hard. She must be as scared as I am."

I stroke her hair and kiss her forehead. "Hold on, little Mama. We'll get you out of this soon. It's a good thing you're not due for another month."

She nods in agreement. "I would be scared to death otherwise."

Charles rises from the couch and moves to the window, pulling back the curtain to inspect the damage.

"It's still dumping snow," he says. "I've never seen a storm like this before."

Julia winces again, this time placing one hand on her stomach and the other on her spine. She gasps and then grunts.

"It hurts too much," she says. "That wasn't a kick. It was something else."

I grip her hand. "What do you mean? Like a contraction?"

She grits her teeth. "I don't know. It's a sharp pain."

Charles leaves the window and rushes to the couch. "Are you okay, honey? What do you need?"

She waves him off. "I'm fine. I'm sure it's nothing—"

A scream belts out of her mouth. Charles and I freeze, stunned.

Julia's breathing becomes rapid. "What's happening?"

I touch her forehead with my hand. It feels like fire.

"You're feverish," I say.

She moans, as another spasm of pain wracks her body. "Am I going into labor?"

I watch her squeeze her legs together and clutch her abdomen.

"Charles, go get some towels," I say. He stares at me without moving. "Go now, please!"

He swallows hard, then races out of the room.

"Let's lay you down, Sissy," I say.

She nods in the middle of another wave of pain. Her petite figure squirms. I remove all the couch cushions, leaving one pillow for her head. She tries to position herself comfortably, but her long dress keeps catching on her sweating legs.

"Why is this happening now?" she asks, her voice feebler than before.

We lock glances. "I'm not sure, but I'm going to take care of you."

The dress fabric around her inner thighs soaks through. Her expression grows murky with terror. "What was that?"

My heart spirals into panic, but I try to stay composed. "I think your water just broke."

***

Two hours later, I am crouched between Julia's knees on the couch, trying to ignore her piercing screams.

"Lainey, it hurts! It hurts!" she bellows, her high-pitched voice echoing through the rooms.

"I know, Sissy, I know," I say. "You have to push. Push *hard.*"

Charles stands at her side, clenching her hand.

"I love you, Julia," he says. The fear drips from his voice. "You can do this. You need to push, like Elaine says."

Julia gasps, covered with sweat. "But she's early. I'm not due for another month. Something's wrong, I can feel it. Something's wrong with her!"

"She's fine," I say, nearly shouting. "She will be all right, but you have to push her out to me."

Charles kisses Julia. "I love you. Stay with me."

"Why does it hurt so much?" asks Julia.

"Push!" I scream.

"Do what she says, Julia," says Charles, stroking the sweat-soaked hair out of her face. "Just focus on how happy we're going to be."

The howling wind blasts the house again. We trade concerned stares. The intensity of the storm is growing.

Charles' voice shakes. "It sounds like the wind is ripping off part of the roof."

I shoot him a warning glare. "Let's not talk about that right now, Charles. Help Julia."

He acknowledges my admonition and clutches Julia's pale hand even tighter. She cries out, as she thrashes on the couch.

"Hold still, Sissy!" I holler, gripping her spread knees. "Push!"

She grunts and then screams, her agony like a vise-grip. The doors rattle on their hinges while the sound of glass shattering rings in my ears.

Tears flood Julia's face. "It's all wrong. Something's wrong!"

The house shudders and groans, the wicked winds continuing to assail it. The roof buckles from the impact of bulky snow descending. Shivering drafts blow through cracks in the walls, winding through the house and over our bodies like the chilling fingers of a ghost.

Suddenly, Julia's voice erupts in a blood-curdling call unlike the others. The sound cuts through me. I reach to grasp the crown of the child's head, believing this latest spasm of her body to be a final, desperate push. Instead, what I am holding is bloody, the red substance pouring out and staining the white couch fabric in a widening pool.

"You're all right, Julia," I say, feeling my throat constrict even as I say the words. "You're going to be fine."

"It hurts too much!" she exclaims, her voice alarmingly weak. "Something's wrong, Sissy. Please, help me."

Tears flow down my cheeks. "I won't let anything happen to you," I say, as calmly as I can. "I'm here. Nobody will hurt you."

Julia shrieks, gasps for breath, and then transfixes on me with frightening focus. "Lainey, promise me you'll take care of my baby."

I stare at her, aghast. "Don't talk that way, Julia. You're going to be fine."

Her eyes grow glassy and she strains to push. "Just promise me. Promise me that you'll take care of her—my little Lisa—no matter what happens."

I crawl around her and lay my head against hers. Tears cascade freely.

"I promise. I love you, Sissy," I whisper.

Julia manages a weak smile and kisses my forehead. "I love you too, Sissy."

Then another scream, this one as strong as the punishing wind pounding the walls of the feeble house.

***

I stare at the white, bloodstained couch in the living room in disbelief. My fingers rub the fabric of my favorite pink sweater as if trying to wipe away the fresh red stains smeared across it. The scene is surreal. I am not here. This cannot be happening. Sissy must be sleeping somewhere in the house.

A newborn's cries assault my ears. Charles appears from the hallway, holding a writhing bundle, trying to stifles her cries by rocking her back and forth in the crook of his arm. His face is gaunt and crimson. He labors to breathe with continuous wheezing.

"You need to take her," he says, extending the bundled mass toward me.

"I don't want to," I say, withdrawing.

"But I'm sick," says Charles. "I've been trying to dig a path through the snow for two days, and I have a bad fever. You need to watch her now. You have to take care of her. You can use the bottles in the kitchen to feed her. Please, Elaine. I can't do it. I don't want her to catch my fever."

I clench my teeth behind closed lips as tears well up. I shake my head at the pathetic, helpless child. "I hate her. I hate what she reminds me of."

"Please, I beg you," he persists. "It's the only way she'll survive. Seclude yourself in your bedroom, away from me, and you can tend to her until the snow melts and we can get help."

"But she's not my baby," I say with a biting tone.

"She is now," he says, stepping forward and thrusting the bundle into my arms. "Do it for Julia."

My promise to her resonates like a thunderclap. Reluctantly, I support the squirming lump, slink past Charles—who coughs wretchedly—and walk with heavy steps toward my quarters.

***

The house is eerily quiet. The snow piled against the windows nearly blocks the sunlight. Propped on the rocking chair, I lean back and forth in rhythm, watching the slumbering baby nestled in my arms. She finally cried herself to sleep after I force-fed her a bottle. I have not moved a muscle since then, hoping her terrible screams will abate this evening.

When I gaze at her, this pitiful thing—Lisa—, I find no bittersweet sentiment—only bitterness. In her innocent features, I see Julia dying. I feel only sadness, not joy, about this new life resting in my arms.

As the minutes pass, something compels me to search the main portion of the house. Charles has not knocked on the door to check on me for more than a day, nor have I heard his hoarse cough echoing through the walls. With caution, I maneuver out of the room, down the hallway, to the living room. The rooms are streaked with shadows—the chilling atmosphere is impossible to warm.

As I enter the living room, I see Charles' bluish, lifeless body sprawled across the white, bloodstained couch. His stare is far off, and his limbs are stiff. The stench of decay gags me, and I turn away.

I hurry back down the hall to my room and place the baby—still blissfully asleep and unaware—onto my bed. I swaddle her with bed sheets and surround her with pillows, then close the bedroom door behind me and prop open the back door off the living room. The door gives way easily thanks to Charles' snow excavating efforts. A ten-foot radius around the doorway is clear, but a wall of packed snow several feet tall stands beyond. I retrieve a blanket from the linen closet and return to the living room.

Spreading the blanket across the floor by the couch, I coerce Charles' body onto the blanket. I struggle to drag him across the hardwood floor and into the backyard, resting him beside the freshly dug mound of earth where Sissy now rests. With trembling hands, I shovel snow onto Charles. I do not have the strength to bury him now. Once he is covered, I rush inside, rubbing my hands to restore feeling into them. With the dread of duty to fulfill my promise, I return to my bedroom to the child.

As I pick up the slumbering burden and hold her to my chest, I stare at her, hatred rising within me. I cannot touch this murderous wretch anymore, so I put her back onto the bed.

She's hurt you, Lainey. A deeper hurt than you could ever imagine. She has taken Sissy and Charles away, and now she wants you to take care of her. This squirming, screaming baby has ruined your family and killed everyone you love. Tell me, what exactly are you going to do about that?

"No, I can't hurt her," I say, rubbing my wrists together. "I won't hurt her."

I pace the room, back and forth, back and forth, back and forth. Tears flow freely like melting snow. I run my hands through my hair, tugging at the unwashed strands until my scalp aches.

Punish her for what she did. You know how to punish her.

"I promised Julia I would take care of her, not hurt her," I whisper, staring at the child.

I leave the bedroom and go to the library, where I close the door and lock myself inside. My breathing is rapid, chaotic. After wiping my cheeks dry, I crawl to the floor and curl up. The pain, bottled up within me, is pressurized and unbearable. I want to pierce something, so I can release it.

You planted precautionary measures for this reason. Use them.

"Not on her," I say. "I won't use the knife on her."

Then use it on yourself, Lainey, or are you even too squeamish for that?

I gnash my teeth and smash my face against the cold hardwood floor. Using both hands, I press down as hard as I can, trying to burst my brain. Julia's image appears, twisted with anguish. More tears flow.

With a scream, I lift myself from the floor to the desk. My shaking hands send books, papers, and pictures flying. I then bolt to the bookcases, pulling them down like dominos, imagining one will land on me and crush me. Somehow, I dodge the falling cases, watching them crash and scatter my precious books across the floor. I fall to my knees and strike my fists against the book covers until my knuckles bleed.

Go in there and finish it.

I dig through the pile of books until I find a knife. I hold it against my wrist and fixate on the glint of the blade, the cold steel on my skin, the promise of escape. I am entranced. It would be so easy to let go with a single slice.

Punish the little, terrible baby first.

Stumbling to the door, I unlock it and return to my bedroom. The child is still sleeping, still clueless about the damage she has caused. I inch closer to the bed, gazing from the flawless face to the shiny knife. I lay next to her, leaning the knife across her forehead. Blood from my knuckles drips onto her skin.

Do it now. You'll be free.

I bounce the knife against the baby's forehead, as if it were a play toy. Then I turn the blade down.

That's it. Finish your revenge.

As I press the blade against her throat, she stirs and yawns, stretching her tiny arms toward me. For a moment, I see Julia—not the image of dying Julia, but the image of my living Julia—sweet, innocent, lovely. A reflection of that cherished person resides in this child—my sister, my best friend, my blood.

Something within me gives way, softening.

I draw the knife away from her—she's no longer a "thing"—she's my niece. The knife falls to the floor. I wipe the blood from her forehead and give her a kiss. We lay together as I shed tears over her fragile frame.

After a while, she stares up at me. As I stare back at her, I realize that my beloved sister lives on in this child. Julia is alive, and she will stay with me as long as Lisa is alive. Now I know why I must become a mother to this baby—not for me, not even for my niece, but for Sissy.

***

Two days have passed, and we remain cut off from the world. After the firewood ran out yesterday, I rounded up all of the pillows, cushions, and blankets from the house and built a barricade around us in my room. We have huddled together, trying to keep warm ever since. I can see our breaths in the dark room—mine a husky fog, hers a tiny cloud.

I still wear the pink sweater, which is now stained red. Somehow, I hope if I keep wearing the sweater, perhaps this nightmare will disappear and pleasant memories of Sissy will return.

If only I can hold tightly to her perfect gift—this pink sweater that she gave me on our birthday last year—she might come back to me.

The food and water supply is disappearing rapidly. I will only have enough to survive for a couple of days. Days ago, snow collapsed the roof above the kitchen, making it impossible to reach the pantry. Part of me hopes the weighty ice will collapse the roof above us as well and end our misery.

Although I continue to bottle-feed her milk, she seems to be hungry all the time. She sucks the bottle dry every time, yet she is still losing weight. She probably wants to die as much as I do. Life has been cruel to her, just as it has been to all the James women.

To resist temptation, I gathered all the knives and buried them in the snow near Julia and Charles. Otherwise, I might have used one of them for both our sake's. If we make it out of this alive, which I doubt we will, I have resolved never to tell her of what happened in this house. Some things children should not know, even when they become adults.

After reading parts of *Jane Eyre* and *Wuthering Heights* aloud to her, I set the books aside and just hold her, waiting for the inevitable. She lay beside her dying mother when she entered the world, and soon she will lie beside my dead body when she leaves it.

***

My stomach stopped growling two days ago, after the food was already gone. I sipped the last of the water last night, allowing its precious drops to linger on my tongue. The baby—Lisa, as I have finally allowed myself to call her—guzzled the last of the bottled milk this morning. The time to die is drawing nearer.

Clutching her to my chest, I scan the room wearily. My strength is gone. Every limb weighs thousands of pounds. My lungs are icy. I want to kiss the baby's forehead, but I resist. I don't want the last person I kiss to be something that I also kill.

Go get a knife, Lainey. Purge the pain. Release her from this hellish reality. Free yourself.

"I don't want to die in here, baby," I say aloud, glancing at my niece. "It's going to be slow and painful if we stay. I'll make it quick for us, I promise. I'm so sorry."

Mustering up all the energy I have left, I struggle to stand, gripping the child against me. Stepping forward, I push through the barricade of pillows, cushions, and blankets with my free hand and unlock the door. I leave my bedroom for the final time and stagger into the hallway, using the wall for balance. Each step is exhausting and every muscle burns. I manage to wobble across the hallway to the living room.

The baby sleeps as I survey the wreckage. Since I last saw it, the living room ceiling has caved in, destroying furniture and leaving mounds of snow everywhere. Where the snow has melted, inches of standing water remain. As I creep along the only wall left unscathed by the avalanche, my feet are soon soaked and frigid.

The sun shines into the roof-less room, blindingly bright compared to the darkness of my bedroom. I jar open the back door to find the entire landscape now covered by only a few inches of white. My attention is drawn to the collection of knives resting near Charles' blue body.

The melted snow does not matter, Lainey. Grab a knife and finish it.

I stare at the glinting blades, feeling the hypnotic pull.

The baby whimpers in my arms. Her cry wakens something maternal in me, powerful and protective.

No, Elaine. I'm getting us out of here. I'm saving us. It's what Julia would have wanted.

I head back inside, making my way to the kitchen to find food. I will need strength to bury the baby's father and lead us to safety. Sissy is relying on me to rescue her daughter, and I can't fail her.

***

Two hours later, as the midday sun looms overhead, my heart breaks all over again as I peel off the bloody pink sweater and lay it to rest on top of Sissy's grave. Then I dress myself in black. The color in my world is gone.

I wrap the crying child in a sling around me. I look for a final time at the mounds of earth where my beloved Sissy and brother-in-law will sleep forever side by side before I head toward the city. My last view of the house reveals that entire sections have disappeared into rubble. Mangled rods, shattered windows, and broken walls have formed a heap that no longer resembles a home. The storm has taken everything, inside and outside.

For hours, as I trudge toward civilization, I want to give up and lie down. My lungs burn, my chest aches, and my joints throb. Each breath I take feels like I'm swallowing an ice cube whole. The snow has stopped, but the wind whips us from all sides. I shield the baby with the sling fabric. Her endless screams turn into white noise, and I no longer hear them as we struggle forward.

Take the baby into town and drop her on someone's doorstep. Sneak away, free of the burden. She's a murdering little wretch. Give her what she deserves.

The uneven road is rough on my swollen feet. The shin-deep snow seems impassable at times. A misstep turns my ankle, and I collapse to the roadside, landing on my tailbone with a thud. The baby screams louder.

Leave it here now, Lainey. On the road. Take off the sling, wrap it up, and walk away.

Tears fall, turning to ice on my cheeks. I grit my teeth and struggle to stand.

I'm saving her. This is what Julia asked me to do. You go to hell, Elaine. I'm not giving up.

I continue toward the city, and soon I can see the shapes glimmer of buildings in the distance.

***

The sun's reflection on the snow in downtown Traverse City blinds me. The baby whines about her difficult life again. I sigh, run a hand through my stringy hair, and rock her back and forth to quiet her. Her screaming intensifies. Exasperated, I readjust the sling to shield her from the frigid wind, and cautiously continue down the slippery sidewalk.

We weave among men in suits and men in tattered rags. Women in fluffed dresses with umbrellas tiptoe along the sidewalk, trying desperately not to ruffle their expensive garments or spot their shoes with snow slush. Model Ts slide down the street, the drivers trying not to lose traction on the black ice. City workers scrape and fling snow off the sidewalks, while others along the walkway sprinkle salt from buckets.

Soon we arrive at the bank, a red brick building with smudged windows. Surprisingly, I hear no cries from the baby in my arms. After stomping my soaked shoes on the welcome carpet, I enter the elegant lobby with its marble floors, teller windows, and executive desks. Mustering courage, I stride straight ahead as if I know where I am going. I glance right and left, nodding to passing strangers who scrutinize me snobbishly at the sight of my baby baggage.

A well-groomed man in a trendy black suit in his mid-thirties steps to my side. With doting brown eyes, prominent cheeks and nose, a wide smile filled with kindness, and dark brown hair slicked to the side, he is appealing indeed.

"Can I help you, Miss?"

A strange calm comes over me. He seems pleasant and attentive.

"I'm a little lost," I say, trying not to sound flustered.

He sees the child in my arms and smiles. "Are you looking for someone in particular?"

I shrug. "I'm not sure. I'm in a bizarre situation. Who would I talk to about the state of finances for someone who has recently passed away?"

"Actually, that's me." He extends his hand. "I'm Paul Jeanetta."

"Elaine James," I say, taking his hand and accepting the comforting grip he offers.

"Please, follow me," he says.

I follow him down a hallway and around a corner to a secluded office with simple, tasteful furniture. He motions toward one of the chairs, and I seat myself as he circles around the desk and eases himself into the high-back chair.

"How old is your child, Mrs. James?" he asks with an interested grin.

I blush. "It's *Miss* James. And the child—well—she's not mine."

"Are you watching her for someone?" he asks.

I sigh involuntarily. "That's part of my bizarre situation, Mr. Jeanetta. Both of her parents died a few days ago after she was born."

His expression shifts to one of shock and sadness. "I'm so sorry," he says.

I avert my gaze, not wanting to cry. "Thank you. I'm sorry too." I glance back at him, seeing his concern that goes beyond job-related responsibility. "The reason I'm here is because I know that her father's investments were linked to this bank. The house he owned in the country was destroyed by the recent snow storm, but I don't know about the rest of his money."

"What was his name?"

"Charles Newark."

He leans forward, his interest piqued. "The hotel owner?"

I nod.

His shoulders slump. "I knew him. He was a friend. We often had lunch together with other business people in town. Charles was a good man."

I bite my lower lip. "Yes, he was a very good man, and he loved my sister very much."

He gawks. "*You're* the twin sister of Julia?"

"Yes," I reply.

"Charles always talked about Julia—though I never met her in person—and he mentioned she had a twin sister."

I smile sadly. "That's me."

His fingers fumble on the desk. "I can't believe he's dead. And your sister as well. I can't tell you how sorry I am. How did it happen?"

Tears well up with a burning sensation. "He caught a fever. He was trying to dig us out from the blizzard. My sister—she—went into labor unexpectedly and—she didn't survive the birth."

We sit in silence. Because of his obvious compassion, I feel I should comfort him after the tragic news. He expels a deep breath, as if to compose himself, and then he opens his hands, palms upward.

"Miss James, this is more than anyone should have to bear alone. I'm going to help you in any way I can. If you don't mind waiting here for a few minutes, I'll review Charles' accounts. Have you eaten lunch?"

I shake my head. "No."

He rises and circles around the desk to my side. "You mentioned the house is destroyed. Do you have anywhere to stay?"

"No," I repeat, my voice quivering.

He nods with urgency. "Don't worry, Miss James. We're going to take care of you and the baby."

"Thank you," I blurt in amazement.

He places a hand on my shoulder. The warmth of his touch gives me solace. "Do you mind waiting for a few minutes?"

"Not at all," my voice squeaks.

"I'll be right back," he says.

He hurries through the doorway and down the hall.

***

Three hours later, I try to process Mr. Jeanetta's words. The remnants of lunch and stacks of papers clutter his desk. He addresses me kindly.

"The police will be exhuming the bodies and taking them for medical examination to verify the causes of death. This is a necessary formality. The house will probably be leveled because it is practically unusable now. Once the insurance company settles the claim, there will be a substantial value assessed for the property."

I place a hand to my forehead.

"Do you have a wife and children, Mr. Jeanetta?" I ask, finally asking the question that has been burning in me since I walked into his office.

He shakes his head. "No, Ms. James, I don't. Why?"

"I was just wondering why you've shown such consideration for me. You knew Charles, but you don't know me."

"I've lost people I've loved before," he says. "And Charles always spoke very highly of you."

We seem to share an understanding, a common residue of pain. To my surprise, I allow myself to be vulnerable to him. As we sit together, I feel an odd, sudden attraction to him. Unlike the other cold, calculated suits in the bank building, he is warm and pleasant.

Suddenly, he snaps awake as if from a dream and rummages through the papers on his desk.

"I want to do what I can for you and this child," he says.

I can't stop the tears from welling up. "Mr. Jeanetta, you are so kind. Are you always this charitable to your clients?"

A sheepish smile crosses his lips. "No, I suppose not. But you seem special to me."

I glance away to hide my embarrassment. "You are making me flustered, Mr. Jeanetta. I didn't expect such generous treatment."

"Please, call me Paul."

"All right. I'm Elaine."

"Elaine—that's a very pretty name. And you have a very pretty face as well."

We both blush.

"I'm sorry," he says. "That was inappropriate."

Our gaze meets, and I smile, feeling strangely emboldened. "It was a compliment. That's never inappropriate."

He smiles, then rubs his hands together as if transitioning back into work mode. "Well, as I mentioned before, I will make arrangements to iron out the sale of Charles' hotel and other business investments. Looking through his records, I noticed that he recently updated his will to transfer all monies associated with his estate to his child in the event of his and Julia's deaths. Should their deaths occur before the child is eighteen, the will states that all monies are to be transferred to you to share with and manage for the child until she turns eighteen. Once we secure death certificates, I will see to it personally that all the details are expedited and that you receive the full amount due to the child. The whole process may take a little while, but you can depend on me to take care of everything."

"Thank you, Paul. You keep amazing me." My heart thumps in my chest. For a moment, I worry that its racing beats will awaken the baby. "I'm very glad I met you."

His reply is reassuring. "Elaine, I wish we could be meeting under different circumstances, but I couldn't be happier that we've crossed paths."

We seem to share a feeling of mutual attraction, but I snap back to reality when I am reminded that I am holding a child in my arms.

"Are you all right?" he asks. "You look a little pale."

"I'm just—overwhelmed by all this," I say.

"Allow me to assist," he says, leaving his chair and helping me to my feet. "The streets are dreadful outside. I will take you wherever you want to go."

I shake my head, still dazed. "You don't have to—"

"It would be my pleasure," he says.

"But I have nowhere to go," I say, with an ashamed whisper.

"Well—I was thinking—" he begins, as if still deciding in his mind how to proceed. "I have a spare room in my apartment if you would like to use it until the hotel sale is completed. I realize it seems forward of me, and I certainly don't want to imply anything other than offering you a place to stay and care for the little one. You can come and go as you wish. I just want to make sure you're taken care of."

I stare at him, bewildered. "Are you serious?"

He certainly looks sincere. "Of course. If you think that seems improper or uncomfortable, I can arrange for you to stay at a hotel instead. I just thought an apartment already stocked with food and other necessities might be more suitable."

Somehow, I sense safety with Paul. "I don't understand. You'd turn your life upside down for a stranger?"

His smile calms me. "You're not a stranger. You're my friend's sister-in-law, you've had to go through something horrific, and now you have to care for your sister's child. The least I can do is to offer you my spare room."

"Are you sure?" I repeat, still stunned.

He grabs his jacket from the coat stand in the corner. "If you'd like, I can take you there now, so you'll be able to rest?"

"I—I—well—" I stammer. I gaze at him again, and my anxiety melts in a moment. "I would love that."

***

The baby, Lisa, who has not been fussy since this morning before the bank visit, sleeps on the bed, swaddled by a blanket, abandoned to dreams. Paul and I sit on opposite sides of the small wooden table in his kitchen. Our coffee mugs are half full, no longer steaming. The refreshing scent of the coffee still lingers in my nose. My body relaxes at last, enjoying the homey surroundings. The apartment includes a narrow living room with a green couch and two tan armchairs, two nice-sized bedrooms on either side of the living room, and a convenient bathroom adjacent to what will be my room.

"Can I be honest with you?" I ask.

"Of course." His voice is warm.

"Besides Julia and Charles, no one has ever been so kind to me. Letting me and Lisa stay here is far more than I deserve."

He shakes his head. "I think it's exactly what you deserve, although I wish I could give you more. You've endured an incredibly painful ordeal, and it shouldn't seem unnatural for me to take you in."

I blush. "But it *is* unnatural. No one else would have done this for me."

He smiles. "I wouldn't have given them the chance because I found you first."

We sit in silence for several moments. I stare at the far wall and rub my wrists together beneath the tabletop.

"I need to tell you something, Paul. Something I feel very guilty about. It will probably change your impression of me, but I need to share it with you."

"I won't judge you, Elaine."

I wipe the tabletop with my hands, as if trying to cleanse it. "I'm having trouble loving Lisa. Every time I see her, she reminds me of what happened to my sister. All my anger, all my grief and pain, is wrapped up in her. To me, her face is my sister's, screaming in agony, asking what is wrong, knowing that something terrible is hurting her."

My voice vanishes, swallowed into my throat as tears form.

"You can tell me," he says. "It's safe with me."

"It sounds horrible," I say, "but I want to treat Lisa badly. I want to punish her for what she made me experience. I realize it's not her fault, but I can't help blaming her. I'm not sure I'll ever be able to forgive her or think of her as *my* child. My heart tells me I'm fulfilling a promise to my sister, but my head tells me I should give her away and free myself. You must think I'm terrible."

He thinks about my words while stealing a sip from his mug. "I think you're grieving, Elaine, as you should. One of my cousins was killed last year—a cousin I was extremely close to. She was struck by an automobile. I was angry for months. I wanted to punish the driver, to track him down and hurt him. I know it's not the same as your situation with the baby, but I understand the feelings involved."

"Even rage?" I ask.

"Yes, especially rage."

I bite my lower lip. More moments pass in heavy silence.

"So, you're not uneasy about sheltering a woman in my predicament?" I ask.

"You mean a woman who is properly grieving the loss of her family and who is rightfully struggling to accept a baby who's not hers? No, I'm not uneasy. In fact, I feel privileged."

We both seem more at ease now that we have shared our separate truths.

"I hope I can work through the sadness of missing Julia," I say. "It's like a crushing weight on my chest."

"You will," says Paul. His hands extend across the table, nearly touching mine but stopping at a respectful distance. "I'm someone you can talk to if you need it."

I brush away tears and smile at him. "Thank you. I don't really know you, but you seem trustworthy. You won't hurt me or the baby."

He nods. "You're right. I won't hurt you or Lisa. If it will put you at ease, here's some of what you don't know about me. I was born and raised here in Traverse City. My parents moved to Chicago last spring. My father was a banker, so I became a banker. My mom volunteered at the soup kitchen downtown, and I loved helping her when I was growing up. I have a few close friends from work, and I live a quiet life. I'm not rich, but I'm happy."

He smiles with an honest, what-you-see-is-what-you-get expression. Without thinking, I suddenly scramble from my seat and reach over to kiss him. Our lips connect with a burst of passion. My tears flow freely as chaotic emotions barrage my heart.

"I'm sorry, I just had to," I say, catching my breath.

He laughs. "You'll never have to apologize for *that*."

He kisses me in return, and I feel that I have come home.

***

The room is peaceful, and it takes me a while to realize that I have not heard the voice in my head for days. No, for months. What is this new, healthy state of being? I smile, sitting on the green living room couch beside Paul, while the little one nestles between us.

The scent of pot roast cooking in the kitchen permeates the air. I touch his fingers, and he clasps my hand. The baby coos and squirms, smiling at us. My heart has been thawing to her. I am growing accustomed to thinking of her as Lisa, rather than as "the murdering thing." However, it may still be a while before I can consider her to be my daughter.

"How are things at the bank?" I ask.

Paul chuckles. "Is that what you really want to talk about?"

"I'm just curious. That's all."

He runs his fingers up my arm. "Boring, as usual. It's hard to concentrate on work when I know you're here."

I smirk. "We've only been together for six months, Paul. Surely you're not that sold on me?"

He nods. "Guilty."

His wandering fingers reach to the back of my head and pull me in for a kiss.

"Guilty again," he says with a smile.

Something in his countenance tells me I am no longer alone in the world. I will have to wait to see if that remains true. Cruelty isn't forgotten easily.

Paul takes a deep breath. He wipes his palms on his dress pants, something I only see him do when he is nervous.

No, not this. Not now.

"I've been thinking about us," he says, unable to meet my gaze. "Our situation is a bit—complicated."

He pauses. A deadly pause.

"Okay," I say. My voice is hollow.

His hands are shaking a bit. "I'd like to simplify it."

Run, Lainey. Run now.

"What do you mean?" I ask.

He fixes his gaze on me. "I would like you to be my wife if you'll have me."

Then, just as I always imagined in my fantasies, he slides off the couch and lowers to one knee. He retrieves a sparkling ring from his pocket and extends it.

"Elaine James, will you marry me?"

Tell him no. Refuse him. Run away. He wants to chain you and take away your freedom. He will hurt you. But you will hurt him more. He's not safe with you. Run.

Tears form as I accept the ring. "Yes," I say quietly.

Paul beams as he places it on my finger. He reaches up to kiss me.

"I have another surprise for you," he whispers.

He dashes into the kitchen and digs through his briefcase, returning with an envelope.

"What's this?" I ask.

He grins. "Open it."

I break the seal and remove a check and a key. It takes a minute for my mind to register the amount printed on the check, made out to me.

"The *Daydream Inn* sold," says Paul, "along with Charles' other investments. Just this week. I was hoping the check would come today."

"This must be a mistake," I say. "The amount—it's too much."

"It's yours and Lisa's. Congratulations, Elaine, you're a rich woman."

The numbers on the check, specifically the multiple zeros, blur for a moment. Then the shiny key catches my attention.

"What's the key for?"

He bends down to my level. "Our new home."

I glance between the key and his elated expression. I am dumbstruck.

Run, Lainey. Get away while you still can. Break his heart now before you break his body later. What he doesn't know about you will kill him. Your secret will destroy him.

I wrap my arms around his neck and pull him toward me. Beside us, Lisa joins in the celebration, giggling to herself, as if she already knows my secret.

***

I stand at the altar, reciting vows to the handsome man facing me. He is exactly the husband I would have picked for myself in my dreams years ago, when such a thing seemed impossible. Eighteen-year-olds are allowed to hope, and the hope I had held to myself in the house with the red stain that would never come clean has finally found and delivered me. I am getting married, and I should want nothing more.

Paul is devastatingly handsome in his black tuxedo. I marvel at the glorious white wedding gown embracing me, the same design as Julia's wedding gown. For a moment, I believe I might have the chance to be whole—for Sissy's sake. She would have wanted this for me.

Then I glance into the crowd of unfamiliar faces, seeing only Paul's family and friends. I have no one to represent me, except the whining baby on the front row being cradled and shushed by one of Paul's friends. The crowd smiles and cries, enamored with the romance of the ceremony. I look back at my fiancé, who has just become my husband.

"I do," and I am done. We are finished with our separate lives. Now we will commence into the impenetrable darkness of the future together like sleepwalkers, side by side, groping for our bearings, having no idea what joy might come beaming through the shadows or what pain might be waiting to swallow us. As we hold hands and sweep down the aisle, blowing and catching kisses, a pain swells inside me. I search for Julia in the crowd. I reach out, hoping she will appear and touch my hand to let me know she is all right and fulfilled to know I have a chance to be happy at last.

But she is gone, and I am alone.

At the reception, I eat, drink, mingle, smile, and blush. I am the perfect bride. I am Paul's splendid new wife, Elaine, the poised, polished queen. But I am not Lainey. I feel separated from my real self. I spin on the dance floor, tease, flirt, and kiss Paul passionately. Joy radiates from us like the sun's rays.

Then something changes with stomach-turning awareness. Elaine James is now Elaine Jeanetta. The James part of me is gone. I have lost my uniqueness. Now I am someone's wife, someone's mother. I am no longer independent *me*. As Julia once did, I have forfeited my womanly name for security with a man.

Sissy, I'm sorry. I've given up our name, the reminder of who we are. What have I done?

The haze overtakes me. All the faces become the same, a single visage, screaming in anguish, ghastly with creeping death. Sissy looms in my mind, asking me why it hurts, what is wrong, will I take care of the creature that is emerging from her womb and killing her. Dizziness follows, then collapse, then strong hands carrying me, splashing water onto my cheeks, cooling me, and holding me until the weeping eventually stops hours later.

During the honeymoon, I am disconsolate. Everywhere I turn, Julia's image appears. How can I enjoy my own happiness when hers was stripped from her? Each intimate expression with Paul transforms into a haunting memory of my sister. Each kiss is laced with guilt because Julia can no longer kiss her husband. Each caress is a reminder of the agony that seized her fragile body before she breathed for the last time. Each evening stroll along the beach is a mental walk to the mound of earth outside the ravaged house where she was buried. Every joy returns me to her deepest pain. Her death has become the lens through which I see my own life.

She is gone, and I am alone.

***

A seismic shift has significantly altered the landscape of my life. After only a few months in our new home, Paul has received a substantial promotion to oversee one of the bank's southern branch offices that called for relocating to Chattanooga, Tennessee. So in spring of 1942, we pack our belongings, travel south to a land of strange accents, and move into a marvelous house with all the features I could ever want. The change in geography has helped part the clouds of my grief.

***

Now after four years since we arrived in Chattanooga, I am finally moving forward with my life. I decided not to tell Lisa about the inheritance money from her parents. It would be pointless anyway because I had spent the majority of it by the time she was old enough to start talking. It will be my secret. Now is not the time to focus on the past. This is my chance to become the woman I have always wanted to be, and I must work to control my circumstances, rather than allowing them to control me. The pain of Julia's memory remains part of me, but I have found a way to bury it in my heart, so although I remember it, it does not sting as before. I welcome the gift of time.

I sit alone, wearing a pink sundress, in my spacious library, twice the size of the one I had before. Ten tall oak bookcases showcase my literary treasures. The matching oak desk displays my favorite hand-made knick knacks from the crafts store downtown, along with several framed family photographs. An end table with an ornate lamp rests between a light blue reading chair and its companion loveseat. The sunlight pays special tribute today, flooding through the open window with kind warmth. I have been devouring *The Woman in White*, finding it compelling as always.

I hear a knock and glance up to see Paul entering, wearing his tailored blue suit and his knowing smile. "Good afternoon, Beautiful," he says.

"Hi, honey. You're home early."

We kiss. How I love this man.

"Just wanted to spend some time with you. Is Lisa still napping?" he asks.

I nod. "She was quite a pill this morning. Ornery little thing."

He chuckles. "Takes after her mother."

An awkward silence follows. Paul leans against the desk, while I remain seated. His expression reveals a difficult conversation brewing.

"What do you need to tell me?" I ask.

He scratches his head. "That fundraiser dinner tonight—do you still want me to come?"

I squint at him. "Of course. That's a silly question. This is important for us."

He sighs. "It's just a bunch of upper-class rich folks throwing money around and congratulating each other on how special they think they are."

I grasp his arm. "It's *important*. How are we going to be respectable here if we aren't willing to rub shoulders with the influential?"

He glances away. "Elaine, we have the big house and the big job—the things you always wanted. Isn't that enough? I just want a simple life for us."

I release his arm. With a cold stare, I turn to my books again.

"That's a simpleton talking," I say. I wait to see if he responds—hoping he will—so I can pounce. But he remains silent.

Smart man. "We are happy here because we have made something of ourselves. We can't risk losing that. I don't want to be homeless, penniless, and friendless again. That's no life."

He groans. "I don't want that for us either, but I'm worried—" He catches himself before completing his thought.

I whirl around to glare at him. "Worried about what?"

He gulps. "Nothing."

I turn back to him and reach out to lift his chin. "You're worried about me, aren't you?"

A sigh escapes his lips. "Yes."

I kiss him and pat his head as if he were a child.

"How sweet. We're going at 6 p.m. sharp. Don't be late."

Before he can reply, I walk away.

***

I stand at the kitchen sink, scrubbing dishes in the hot, soapy water. For a moment, I gaze intently at the white marble countertop, recalling with pleasure how much Paul was willing to pay for it, until an excited voice hollers from the living room.

"Mama, look at my picture!"

Lisa's petite, six-year-old figure bustles around the corner and careens onto the white kitchen tile floor. I smell chocolate on her in an instant. Her black curls bob on her head and the brown freckles on her cheeks complement her little button nose. Her blue jeans have grass stains on the knees and her orange shirt arrayed with pictures of butterflies is grubby from another chocolate snack attack. How she manages to keep finding my constantly relocating secret stash of Hershey's Kisses is beyond me. Sneaky little thing. A piece of paper flutters like a flag in her hand.

"You wanna see it, Mama? You wanna see it?"

"Of course, baby," I say, drying my hands. "But first, what's that on your shirt?"

She shrugs. "I don't know, Mama."

I place my hands on my hips. "It looks like chocolate to me, Lisa."

She stares at me, perplexed. "Chocolate? How did *that* get there?"

I wet a washcloth and clean the residue from her shirt. "That's what I'm asking you, young lady. Where did you get the chocolate?"

Redness flares in her cheeks. "How do *you* think it got there, Mama?"

I hold her chin and struggle not to smile. "I think you got into my personal stash of Hershey's Kisses again and took some for yourself, didn't you?"

She smiles wide. "I *love* chocolate, Mama."

I sigh. "I know you do, Sweetheart, but what did we say about my chocolates?"

She pouts. "'They're not *my* Kisses. They're *Mama's* Kisses.'"

"That's right. Now, are you going to take any more of Mama's Kisses?"

She bites her lip. "No, Mama. I'll be good, I promise."

"That's my girl," I say, kissing her forehead. "So, what's this picture you want to show me?"

Lisa hands the paper to me and waits for my reaction. The picture is amazingly detailed for a six-year-old. A one-story house with two bedrooms, a living room piled high with books, a kitchen, and a basement with a red stain. An old woman claws at her face, which appears to be on fire. Two young girls cling to each other, their mouths open with blue tears running down their cheeks. I gasp and drop the picture.

"What's wrong, Mama?" asks Lisa. "Don't you like it?"

"It's—it's—very nice, baby. How did you—where did you—what is this picture about? Why did you draw this?"

She scoops her masterpiece off the floor, squints at it, and then hugs it to herself. "I didn't draw it, Mama," she says.

I stare at her, rubbing my wrists together, irritating and chafing my skin. "Don't lie to me, Lisa."

She appears frightened. "I'm not lying. I didn't draw it."

I try to grab the paper from her, but she steps away and clasps it against her tiny chest.

"Then who did?" I ask.

She holds up her hands as if the answer is obvious. "You did, Mama."

"What?" I quaver.

She scurries away momentarily and returns with another picture of a larger house covered with snow. In the living room, a female figure lies on a white couch spotted with red. A blue-faced male lies on the floor. A female stands between them, holding a baby. Tears flow suddenly as my skin pales.

"You drew this one too," she says.

My wrists scrape. "When did I draw these?"

She smiles. "Last night. While you were sleeping. You came into my room and sat on my bed. You asked me for my crayons and paper. Then you drew them."

My body stiffens. "I was asleep?"

She nods. "Yes, Mama."

"How do you know I was asleep?"

"Your eyes—they were like this." She gives me a dazed, far off look. "What do the pictures mean, Mama?"

Struggling to keep my hands steady, I give her back the second picture, and she clutches both drawings.

"I—I—don't know, baby," I stammer. "I guess I was dreaming. These pictures aren't real. They don't mean anything."

She watches me with suspicion. "Are you sure?"

"I'm sure, Lisa."

She shrugs. "Okay. Do you want me to hang the pictures on my bedroom wall?"

I feel my cheeks flush. "That's okay, baby. Why don't you give them to me and I'll find a special place for them? Like a hiding place. It will be our secret, and we can't tell anyone about it."

The intrigue of the statement lights in her expression. "Good idea, Mama."

She gives them to me and then claps her hands.

"Why don't you go play in your room, Lisa? If you keep our secret and never talk about the pictures again, I'll give you extra dessert every night for the rest of the week."

She marvels. "You mean ice cream *and* a brownie?"

I smile. "Yes. Now, remember what I said."

Lisa holds her fingers up to her mouth and pretends to seal her lips and throw away the key.

"That's my girl," I say.

She scurries off toward the stairs. Just before rounding the corner out of sight, she turns back to me.

"Mama, I promise I'll be good."

"You're always good, Lisa."

"I know, but I promise I'll be even better so maybe the bad dreams can leave. But if I wake up screaming tonight, I'll scream into my pillow so you won't hear it, just like I always do. Don't worry, Mama, I promise I'll be good."

I stare at her, bewildered. "Lisa, what are your bad dreams? Do you want to talk about it?"

She grins and holds her fingers to her mouth, repeating the motion of sealing her lips and throwing away the key. Before I can respond, she dashes up the stairs and out of sight. An ache throbs in my chest. I grip the drawings in my sweaty hands.

You know what to do, Lainey.

Once I hear Lisa's feet thumping upstairs in her room, I retrieve an old mixing bowl and a long-nosed lighter from the kitchen cabinet. I quickly light the pictures and place them into the sink. The crayon creations melt away, and I cover the fire with the bowl, smothering any smoke or ash that might escape.

After the flame has died out, I flush any remaining evidence down the drain. Still not satisfied, I run the disposal and listen to the result of last night's sleepwalking incident pulverize into oblivion.

Now, what to do about this damned sleepwalking?

***

The night air refreshes as I climb the deck railing and prepare to leap onto the rocks. I hum a song, either a jazz tune from my wedding day or something I just made up. I'm not sure which. For a little while, until I muster the courage to jump, I sit on the railing and enjoy the moonlight reflecting off the lake just beyond the rocky edge. After my song ends, I listen to the soothing breeze coming off the lake. The scent of crisp water fills my nostrils, giving my heart a quiet thrill. It is so peaceful here at this house.

I peer forty feet below to the bottom of the cliff. It's going to be quite a nasty fall, but if Elaine tells me in my head to do it, she must be right. She knows best, after all. She's gotten me this far.

"Elaine!" a voice whispers from behind me and startles me.

I snap to alertness, almost losing my balance on the railing. Behind me, Christina Hunt rushes across her deck to my side.

Her white nightgown accentuates her bleached blonde hair and her pretty, vivacious features that seem ten years younger and much less wrinkled than mine. It takes me a moment to realize I am in my nightgown as well.

"What am I doing out here?" I ask her.

"I was about to ask you the same question. Are you all right?"

She helps me climb to the safe side of the railing.

"I'm sorry," I say. "I was sleeping, I think."

Christina feels my forehead. "You're not feverish. Do you usually sleepwalk?"

I offer a grim smile. "I guess I do."

She leads me to a chair at the deck table. "Let me get you a glass of water."

I wave her off. "No, please don't bother. I'll be fine to go home now."

She sits down across from me and expresses concern. "You should see a doctor if you're sleepwalking to that extent."

I look away. "I'm sure it's nothing."

"Don't give me that, Elaine," she says. "We've been friends for four years now. We can be honest with each other. You got out of your bed, left your house, and walked almost ten minutes to get here and climb my deck railing. That's a lot more than nothing. You can get medication to help. Maybe something that will make you sleep soundly so you won't get out of bed once you lie down."

I give her a skeptical glance. "What do you mean? Like a prescription drug?"

She nods. "Yes. Jeffrey snores like a jet engine, so the doctor gave me sleeping pills to knock me out so I can't hear him. They work like a charm."

I rub my temples, trying to fend off a headache. "I'm not going to a doctor about this."

She mulls my words, then looks away. "Do you want to try some of my pills?"

"Are you sure?" I ask.

"I'm worried about your safety, Elaine. You can't just go wandering around the neighborhood fast asleep. You could have accidentally fallen off my deck railing."

I flinch at this thought. "Okay, I'll try them."

Christina smiles. "Good. I bet they'll do the trick. By the way, does Paul know about the sleepwalking?"

I shake my head.

"What about Lisa?"

My wrists scrape together in the darkness. "Let's keep what happened tonight between us."

"As long as you promise to see a doctor if my pills don't help," she says.

"Okay," I whisper.

Christina grasps my hand and squeezes it. "I'll be right back," she says.

***

Thank God the sleeping pills are working, Elaine. No more sleepwalking chaos for you. I can't believe you would have thrown us over a deck railing onto a bed of rocks.

Oh, Lainey, you're so dramatic. I wasn't going to make us jump. Or was I? I guess we'll never know.

You're sick, Elaine. At least I have subdued you for now. We can't afford to have you sleepwalking, destroying things, and hurting yourself and others.

Lainey, we both know these pills are only a temporary fix. I'll be free soon enough. I'm just biding my time. Besides, who says I need to sleepwalk to do damage?

***

I creak back and forth in the rocking chair, listening to childish giggles nearby. In the corner of the pink-walled playroom, Lisa, now eight years old, sports two pigtails while squatting among scattered wooden blocks. Spaghetti stains cover her navy blue shirt. An hour earlier, after lunch, I ordered her to change her shirt, and she responded by pounding her fists on the floor and screaming until my ears rang. If only Paul had been home—the tantrum would have been diffused in moments. She respects his authority and obeys without question, but she would rather play a game of constant defiance with me.

Once she rose from the floor and stopped screaming, I thought perhaps her fit had subsided. I discovered otherwise when she began pushing over the kitchen chairs and flinging the dirty plates from the table toward the sink, shattering them against the tile wall. A gleeful laugh erupted from her as she caused the destruction. I finally gave up and yelled at her to go to her room. As she trotted away with a crooked grin, I knew the only lesson she'd learn from the episode is that Mama can be defeated and, if she makes enough of a scene, Mama will let her wear her saucy mess of a shirt around the house and do as she pleases. Another defeat today.

An hour after the incident, Lisa bobs her head and hums along to a made-up song. Her clumsy hands paw at the blocks and knock them against each other. Gleefully, she tosses the blocks against the wall, causing scuffmarks on the pink wall. She claps her hands in triumph at her carefully planned wreckage.

"Lisa, stop that," I say.

"I can't, Mama," she says.

I stand and stomp my foot. "Yes, you can. Now stop, or I'll take the blocks away."

She looks at me sincerely. "The lady in the pictures is doing it."

I stare at her. "What did you say?"

She shrugs. "The lady with the fire face. It's her fault. Sorry."

My cheek twitches. "What lady with the fire face?"

"The one in the picture you drew. From a couple of years ago. It was our little secret. I never forgot. Do you remember?"

I stiffen. "No, I don't remember. That never happened. You're imagining things again, Lisa."

"No I'm not," she says, standing and stomping her foot, mimicking me. "You hid the pictures. Where are they, Mama? I want to see them again."

I move to her and hold up my empty hands to show her I don't have them. "Have you seen them in the past two years?"

She crinkles her nose. "No."

I lean down and squint at her. "That's because there are no pictures. There never *were* any pictures."

Her hands slide behind her back. I know she is rubbing her wrists together. "But I remember the old lady with the fire face. I saw her in the picture, and I see her in my dreams."

"Be quiet," I say.

"I remember her!"

"Be quiet!" I say louder.

She backs away from me and scrunches her forehead, devising her next defiant act.

"Mama?"

"What?"

"Do you ever sleepwalk anymore?

"No."

"Do you ever see me sleepwalking at night?"

"No."

"Do you think I will start sleepwalking when I get older?"

"No."

"Why don't you believe in the lady with the fire face?"

I glare at this clever little person always trying to catch me off guard.

"Those are silly dreams, Lisa," I say. "What you can see is all that's important."

"You can't see the lady making me throw the blocks, but she's real to me, Mama."

I grit my teeth. "Stop pretending. It's *you* throwing the blocks and it's *you* who's going to be in trouble, young lady."

She spins around, flinging her arms widely. "I don't want to throw blocks, Mama. The lady makes me."

"There *is* no lady," I say, my tone darkening.

"She's real, Mama! In my dreams, she hits me and hurts me and makes me bad. That's why I get in trouble."

I grip her shoulders and pin her against the wall. "You get in trouble because *you* don't do as I say. Be a good girl and play nicely with your blocks. I won't ask you again."

Her look is one of incredulity. "I don't have any blocks."

"What about those blocks right there?" I ask, motioning toward the heap of blocks on the floor behind us.

"Those are the lady's. She won't let me have any of them."

I sigh. "Lisa, your daddy bought them for you. They're yours, not the lady's."

With a peculiar fire in her voice, she says, "So, you *do* think the lady is real!"

"I didn't say that."

She breaks free of my grasp and dances around me, swinging her head. "You *said* it, you *said* it!"

I grab her arm, twisting it until she stands still.

"That hurts, Mama!" she yells.

"Then stop disobeying me," I demand.

With an odd contempt, we stare at each other. I take a deep breath and try to keep my voice steady.

"Listen to me, Lisa. You are real and I am real, that's all. There is no lady with a fire face. You made her up. Understand? Why can't you just behave and play nice?"

A peevish grin curls on her lips. "I'll never play nice."

"Yes, you will play nice, or else I'm going to tell your daddy about it."

She nervously rethinks her disobedience.

With hands on hips I scan the room. "Why don't you play with Raggedy Ann instead? She's your favorite, right?"

Lisa purses her lips, considering. Then she darts across the room, picks up the red-haired doll from a menagerie of stuffed animals, and hurries back to my side. "Raggedy Ann *is* my favorite, Mama," she says.

I smile with relief. "Good. Now why don't you play with her using a quiet voice?"

Lisa stares at Raggedy Ann. Suddenly, she grabs the doll around the neck and pulls hard, tearing the fabric until the head comes off. My insides contract.

"Lisa, why did you do that?" I ask.

She shrugs and stares at me matter-of-factly. "I'm done with her. Now she's dead." Her demeanor immediately transitions, as if the doll decapitation never even happened. "I hate it here, Mama. Why do we always have to dress up and go to parties and pretend we're nice?"

I try to change the subject. "Stop asking questions."

"Why?"

"Because I said so."

"I don't like you or the lady with the fire face!"

I glare at her. "I don't care what you like or what you don't like. You will obey me or you won't be able to sit down for a week. Do you want the belt, Lisa?" She shakes her head. "Then play with your blocks like a good girl and keep quiet."

"Yes, Mama," she says, as if in a trance. "I will stop talking right now. See, Mama, I'm not talking anymore. This is me not talking, Mama."

I raise my hand toward her, and she cringes.

"Not another word, Lisa."

She makes the usual sealing motion across her lips and throws away the key.

I no sooner turn around when I hear a crashing sound. Whirling around, I see Lisa flinging herself into the wall, knocking her head into the same spot her wooden block had made contact minutes ago. Blood trickles from a gash on her forehead. Her eyes redden and water, but her devilish grin persists.

"Why are you hurting me, Mama?" she asks. "Stop hurting me!"

I stare bewildered.

**

Five more years have passed in a blink.

Little Lisa has become a teenager, a thirteen-year-old witch, her unruliness increasing with each year. Her petite frame is broadening, and her once adorable features—the black, curly hair, button nose, and freckles—have grown unkempt, acne-riddled, and less becoming. A chasm has developed between Paul and me, compliments of Lisa. Her proximity to us breeds contempt for each other. Nowadays, he speaks to me only when he must, blaming the rough edges of our relationship on my "erratic behavior." If only he knew the error of that statement. He has not seen me completely erratic yet. If he had, he would be more circumspect with his words to me.

I do not have time to make amends with a husband who drowns his perceived sorrows in a bottle. I wish to maintain a life endued with power and control, and I will not succumb to being a victim of circumstance, as I was in my weak youth. I need to spend my time listening to my inner guide, the voice that prompts me to action and empowers me to actualize the future I crave. My token husband and petulant daughter are merely obstacles to be overcome. I love them more than life itself, but if they stand in the way of the life I want, no amount of love will keep my wrath at bay.

Perhaps it is time for me to stop taking the sleeping pills and see what happens. Suppressing the sleepwalking is preventing me from living with a sense of power. For many years now, I have drugged myself into being docile. I am weary of being a muzzled dog. I want to run, I want to sniff and explore, I want to bite. I am curious as to what I could do and what I could be if the boundaries were removed. Maybe I should view it as an experiment. Surely, I can control myself now. It's been six years since the last incident. I need to show my strength, and I can only do that by lifting the night fog of my medicated stupor. It's time to set myself free.

Soon they will see that although I am a domesticated woman, I am far from tame.

***

I survey Lisa's room, scowling at the dresser cluttered with what looks like gaudy stage makeup paraphernalia. The bed has wadded, unmade covers, and the white walls are covered with multi-colored, bizarrely designed "artsy" posters which were probably procured from unsavory, bohemian characters at the downtown arts festival.

"Lisa, you listen to me! Take off those rags and put on your dress this minute!"

Lisa cocks her head at me and laughs, patting the tattered black pants and oversized shirt. "You can't make me, Mama. I'm thirteen, and I'll wear whatever I want."

I shake my head and grit my teeth. "I will not have this disobedience in my house. You are going to this party with your father and me, and that is final!"

Lisa lifts her chin and ruffles her nose. "I hate our fake life with those stuffy, wealthy people. Always smiling, always pretending everything's perfect. It's not real, Mama. It's not right."

I sigh and survey her for a moment. "Where did you get those clothes?"

"A friend from school," she says with a shrug.

"What is her name?"

She smiles. "Wesley."

My lip curls. "That's a boy's name."

She nods. "He's my friend. We play in the school band together. He lives across town—in the lower part."

I place my hands on my hips. "Why are you spending time with this boy?"

She smirks. "Because I'm a troubled teenager."

"I don't want you to see him anymore. Understood?"

"No, I don't understand, Mama. What's wrong with having a friend?"

I grip her chin. "Lisa, there's nothing wrong with having a friend. But having a friend who's a boy is something completely different."

She rolls her eyes. "Why?"

I grin bitterly. "Because you're a troubled teenager."

She pushes my hand from her chin and wanders over to her bed, plopping down with dramatic flair. "I don't want to be here anymore. Can't I just stay in my room while you and Daddy have your party?"

"Stop being difficult," I say. "You're in a grown-up house, and you need to act like you belong here. You can't be wearing rags and associating with less-than-worthy boys who live across town in the poor district. We have an image to maintain, and I will not tolerate your tarnishing it."

Her eyes flash angrily. "You just keep me locked up in this prison until you need to show me off for one of your important-person parties. I'm sick of it, Mama. I want to see things, I want to travel, and I want to date boys."

Before I consider the consequences, I march over to her bed and grab her by the collar. My voice slices the air with the precision of a knife. "Get out of these clothes and into your dress or else you're going to regret waking up this morning. You think I won't use the belt this time?"

Tears fall unbidden down her cheeks.

"What's wrong with you, Mama? Why have you been acting so strangely lately?"

"Be downstairs in ten minutes or else," I say, my tone low and menacing.

I release her collar, turn my back on her, and storm out of the room.

***

Lisa is tucked in bed, the lamp on her nightstand casting an eerie shadow across her face. She looks anxious but submissive.

Don't believe her façade, Lainey. She's a deceptively keen actress. See those puppy eyes. Somehow she knows you killed Aunt Verna, and she knows you're not her real mother. She knows everything. She's seen it in her dreams. She will turn on you at the first opportunity.

My expression conveys a mixture of coldness and condemnation. She swallows hard.

"Goodnight, Mama," she says, her voice airy thin. "I'm sorry I gave you a hard time today. The party was very nice."

"Straight to sleep," I say. "No reading, no writing, and no drawing. Understood?"

"Yes, Mama."

Cloudiness creeps through my mind. I glimpse Lisa, but I see Julia writhing in agony instead. My rage rises.

Hurt her, Lainey, because she hurt you. She killed Sissy.

No, Elaine. Stop thinking that way. It wasn't Lisa's fault, remember? You don't hate your daughter.

She's not my daughter! She's a murderous little wretch!

Quiet, Elaine. Walk away. Turn around and walk out of her room before you do something rash.

Clenching my fist behind my back, I move toward the door.

"Mama?" asks Lisa.

My body feels icy. "What?"

"I really am sorry," she says.

I stare at her for a moment, debating whether to thaw or turn the temperature even lower. "Go to sleep," I mutter.

"But I said I'm sorry," says Lisa, her voice verging on desperation. "Can't you forgive me? I won't be able to sleep until I know you're not mad anymore. I said I'm sorry, Mama."

Crush her, Lainey. She crushed you first.

I grit my teeth. "And *I* said go to sleep. Not another word, you hear me? You're in enough trouble as it is. Saying you're sorry doesn't make up for everything you've done."

Tears swim as she pleas, "Please, just say you forgive me."

You can never forgive her for what she did to Sissy.

I shake my head. "This is what you get for being sorry."

I slam the door.

***

Dinner passes with polite banter, and the wine-laced after-dinner conversation begins. The wonderful scent of the roasted duck still lingers in my nose. We sit on the deck of an enormous house built on a cliff nearly forty feet above the rocky lake shoreline. I can faintly hear insects buzzing from the water's edge. This has long been our Thursday night custom with our closest friends. From the deck's banister one can overlook the entire lake, a view worth every penny of the hefty price tag according to the owners. It pays to have friends richer than we are.

Jeffrey and Christina Hunt sit opposite Paul and me at a fancy white wooden table with a sparkling glass top, absorbing the evening's atmosphere. I survey our friends, marveling at their picture-perfect qualities: evenly tanned complexions, shapely noses, cheek bones, and chins, sparkling white teeth, locks of sunny blonde hair, and smiles as strong as their gusto for life. They are the ideal couple, the couple Paul and I could be if only he tried harder. Christina wears a flowing magenta dress, one I could never afford, while Jeffrey dons a blue sports coat, which probably cost as much as any one of Paul's suits. My simple yellow dress and Paul's orange polo shirt seem lackluster compared to our friends' outfits. No matter what we wear in the presence of the Hunts, we will always be underdressed.

Jeffrey raises his glass, filled to the brim with red wine. "To Thursday nights with friends," he says.

We raise our glasses, clink, and sip. Paul does more than sip. I give him a discreet warning glance, but he pretends not to notice.

"Thanks for hosting this week, Christina," I say. "Lisa has been acting out again, I'm afraid. She would have ruined the evening."

Christina smiles. "I guess that is the life of a thirteen-year-old—the ruin of all that is peaceful." She pauses, as if trying to stop herself from speaking, but then she continues. Tears threaten for a moment. "I wish I had a daughter to irritate me. I would do anything for that kind of blessed burden."

I frown. "I'm sorry, dear. I didn't mean to upset you."

She waves me off. "I didn't mean anything by it. You'll have to forgive my self-pity parties when they pop up unexpectedly. It's not as if we didn't try."

Jeffrey reaches over to squeeze her hand. "Let's talk about something else, shall we?"

I nod, and Christina averts her gaze. Paul tops off his wine again.

She clears her throat. "Have you all heard about Mayor Flinder and his wife? She's pregnant."

"Really?" I say. "I had no idea they were trying."

She smiles. "I think it will be a boy."

Jeffrey chuckles. "I bet it's a boy, too. That way, Sam Flinder will have an heir to his throne someday. Nobody will challenge the Flinder family for ownership of this city. After Sam's three terms are up, he'll begin grooming his boy for the position. Yep, my money's on its being a boy. Sam Flinder gets his way every time, so why not with the gender of his unborn child?"

"A valid point," I say. "You sound a bit jealous, Jeffrey. Am I right?"

He grins. "You're not subtle, Elaine. No one will ever accuse you of that. Christina and I may be a decade younger than you and Paul, but we have just as much ambition. I'll admit I've had my thoughts about politics. The business sector suits me well, but the real power lies in politics. The ability to influence and to make decisions that affect people's livelihood intrigues me. It's intoxicating to think about—the magnitude of being in a position like that."

Christina touches his arm as a subtle reminder to stop talking. He doesn't seem to mind her gesture. He's used to it.

"Jeffrey has wild ideas when the wine gets him going," she says.

He waves her off. Then he raises her hand and kisses it.

"I was being serious, but now I guess I'm supposed to be sorry," he says.

Paul is fixated on his glass, swirling the red liquid round and round.

"That's enough, honey," I say, with all the sweetness I can muster. "You'll upset your stomach."

He leans back in his chair and cradles the glass to his chest. "Sorry, I don't have anything to contribute to this conversation."

I pat his leg like a doting mother. "That's all right. We'll keep the chatter afloat just fine without you."

Christina perks up. "I do envy the Flinders. Don't you, Elaine?"

I shrug. "I don't know that I'd want to be in an occupation that has pressure along with power. I think I would just want the power, without any of the responsibility or stress."

Jeffrey chuckles. "You're telling me you wouldn't want to rule over people and help control them? I know you, Elaine. You have the venom of a strong matriarch in your veins."

"Jeffrey!" says Christina, smacking his hand. "That's out of line."

I shake my head. "I'm not offended. I fight to control things. But I would rather control my own world than control others."

"Are you sure about that? You could have fooled me."

It takes me a moment to realize Paul has just spoken.

We stare at him, waiting for an explanation. He stands from his chair and gulps the rest of the wine in his glass.

"Thank you for a lovely dinner," says Paul, dispirited. "I think I'll go home and sleep now."

Christina grasps Jeffrey's hand. "Why don't we go inside and give them a minute, Jeffrey?"

Before I can respond, they disappear into the house. I am alone at the table, watching Paul inch closer to the deck railing, clutching his empty glass.

"Can you explain what just happened?" I ask.

He does not reply, so I stand and walk over to him. I attempt to take the glass from his hand, but he pulls it away. Then with a wry smile, he drops the glass onto the rocks below the deck. It shatters, sending fragments that glint in the setting sunlight.

"That's your explanation," he says.

My insides boil. "Look at me."

He tilts his head in my direction. "What *controlling* question do you have for me now?"

"Why do you keep drinking like this? We're with our best friends, for God's sake. Have some decency. We have a reputation to uphold, or have you forgotten how civilized people are supposed to act?"

He laughs. "I haven't forgotten. I know exactly how I'm supposed to act. That's why I do things like *that* instead." He points to the glass shards below.

I huff and avert my glance. "I can't believe you've turned into a pathetic shadow of a real man. Even with your promotion at the bank, you're still dejected and depressed. Why are you like this?"

He expels a heavy sigh. "I'm having trouble handling it this time."

I cross my arms and glare at him like a strict schoolteacher. "Handling what, Paul? What trivial thing has overwhelmed you now?"

He winces. "You, Elaine. It's been happening again."

"What's been happening?"

When he speaks, his voice lowers. "You've been sleepwalking. Every night I find you tearing up things in the house during a nightmare. Screaming, asking where your knives are hidden. Trying to sneak into Lisa's room, saying you're going to hurt her because she's hurt you. All while you're asleep. You don't even know you're doing it."

I grit my teeth. "That's a lie. I don't believe it."

He sighs. "Of course you don't believe it because you don't remember it. I never sleep anymore because I'm always chasing you around the house, cleaning up your messes, fixing or hiding whatever you've destroyed, and calming Lisa down when you barge in on her with your fists flailing. I can't take it anymore. You need to get help."

I grip the skin on his forearm and squeeze it until the flesh blanches. "Why are you making up these lies about me? If you're depressed, that's your problem, Paul. Deal with it. See a psychiatrist. But don't drag me down with you and pretend I've gone wrong in the head. I won't stand for this. You know I won't."

His laugh is bitter. "Yes, I know you won't. That's my dilemma. I tell you the truth and you turn back at me. I'm your husband, so I'll take whatever crap you have to shovel. But not Lisa. I won't let you terrorize and control her anymore. She's not yours." He glowers at me. "She's not *your* child, remember?"

I smack his cheek and strike him again and again. "Bastard. I'm taking Lisa and leaving you."

He wrestles my arms into submission. "You won't get very far, dear. I'll freeze your assets so you won't be able to access a penny of our money. I'm not vindictive, but I'll do it so you can't hurt Lisa. You're not going to have control. You're going to have to learn to behave and get the help you need. Can't you see how your actions affect others? Congratulations, Elaine. You've single-handedly made me a drunk. That's quite an accomplishment."

"Don't blame me for your shortcomings," I say.

He finally releases my arm and views the glass shards below. "I love you too much to stand by and let you destroy yourself."

I run a hand through my hair, hoping the motion will give me composure. I observe the bruise forming on his arm where my fingers had squeezed. Suddenly, something in me breaks.

"I know," I whisper. "I'm sorry. I'm terrified of myself. I don't know how to fix it."

He places a hand on my shoulder. Not an embrace, just a hand.

"Maybe we should have you start with a sleep doctor," he says.

I grimace. "That won't help."

"Why not?"

Tears form quickly. "Because I still want to do those things even when I'm awake."

His body stiffens.

The door leading to the house opens and Christina's chipper voice greets our ears.

"Is everything all right out here?"

I turn and force a smile. "Yes, we're just finishing up. Sorry for the interruption. I'm afraid we'll need to leave early tonight."

"I understand," says Christina. "Do you want to take dessert with you?"

Paul moves to the table and picks up an unopened bottle of wine. "This is all I need. Thanks."

***

I advance toward Lisa, whose terror has paled her normally rosy cheeks as she cowers on her bed.

"Please, Mama, let me out of here. I didn't do anything. You have to believe me. I didn't hurt someone named Julia. I don't even know who that is."

I grip her wrists and shake her. "I know it was you! You killed her. You dream about it because you remember doing it!"

She recoils. "No, Mama, no. Please, come to your senses. I don't *know* Julia."

Fierce pounding rebounds from the locked bedroom door.

"Elaine!" Paul's voice rings out. "Stop whatever you're doing. Let Lisa go!"

Lisa pleads for me to listen to her father. "Mama—"

"Shut up!" I yell, flames rising in my cheeks. "You were jealous of Julia. You wanted her gone."

"Mama, I don't know what you're talking about."

Pressing my palms to my forehead, I grit my teeth, trying to fend off my dark thoughts. "You knew she was the one I loved most, so you killed her. Now you want to ruin everything else in my life."

Lisa reaches out with a gesture of pseudo-consolation, but I strike her in self-defense. "You hurt her, so I'll hurt you."

Lisa feels her bruised cheek as the pounding at the door continues. She shields her head with her arms. Suddenly, the pounding stops.

I see the image of a burning lamp exploding onto Aunt Verna's face. Then Julia writhes and screams in agony, reaching for me to save her.

"I won't let you hurt me anymore," I say, towering over Lisa's cringing figure.

The door booms with a force stronger than a mere fist. Another pulsing thud, and the door bursts open. Paul throws aside a sledgehammer and rushes to me with his hands raised.

"Elaine, don't touch her. You're not thinking clearly. You don't want to hurt anyone."

I scowl and move toward him, but he enfolds me tightly. I fidget and scream, but he is stronger than me.

"It's okay," he whispers. "Calm down. It's okay. I'm here. I understand. She didn't know Julia. She hasn't hurt anyone. You don't want to hurt her."

"Wake up, Mama!" screams Lisa. "Wake up!"

Consciousness suddenly flicks on like a light switch. I am standing in Lisa's room, being embraced by my husband. Lisa is curled up in a fetal position on her bed. She seems frightened. Why is she so afraid? I relax my tense muscles.

"You don't want to hurt her," says Paul.

"Why would I want to hurt her?" my voice whimpers. "She's my angel."

He kisses my forehead. "Let's not worry about that right now. Let's just go to the kitchen, get something to eat, and talk the whole thing through, all right?"

My sweet Lisa remains in a defensive crouch.

"Lisa, baby, I'm so sorry," I say. "I didn't mean to—"

Before I can finish, she scrambles to her feet and rushes from the room. My heart plummets as I watch her go.

***

I bolt upright in bed, crying in the middle of the night. My insides twist in knots. Paul reaches over to soothe me.

"I hurt her, Paul," I whisper. "I hurt Lisa. I didn't mean to. I must have been sleepwalking again. I'm so sorry. She just reminds me of everything that's painful."

"I know," he says. "But you won't hurt her anymore, right?"

"Of course not. I'll never hurt my baby girl again. I'll keep her safe with me, always."

"Will you promise to schedule an appointment with a psychiatrist this week?"

"Absolutely. I'll do it first thing in the morning."

"Good. I'll ask you about it when I get home from work to make sure you've followed through."

"Yes, that would be smart."

"I don't want you to do anything you'll regret, Elaine."

"I don't *want* to do anything I will regret."

"Good."

"Yes, yes. Very good."

"I love you."

"I love you too."

I lie back down in the darkness and try to sleep.

***

A middle-aged woman with graying hair, a kind countenance, and a modest charcoal-colored pantsuit sits across from me, her legs crossed, her pen and pad of paper ready to pick me apart. I allow my nose to search the room, finding my perfume is superior in scent to hers. I remember the first time I smelled perfume—it was a gift from Charles that Julia wore when she came to tell me she was falling in love with him. The memory creates a lump in my throat, so I fidget on the couch to dismiss the thought and appear unflustered.

"Elaine, we have been meeting for a month now, and I am pleased with your progress thus far," says the woman. Her voice is soft, like a feather.

"Thank you, Mrs. Burke," I say, straightening my posture, smoothing some wrinkles from the nicest pink dress I own, and flashing a cheery smile. "These sessions have helped me immensely."

She nods and makes a note on her pad. "In closing today, let's recap the previous week and focus on progressive methods for next week. Have you been practicing the breathing techniques I taught you for anxiety?"

"Yes, every day."

"Good."

Another note jotted on the pad.

"How have you been feeling? Describe your moods this past week."

I glance around the room, giving myself time to formulate the perfect answer. The light green carpet complements the beige armchair and couch tastefully. Her dark wooden desk has tidy paperwork piles lying face down for privacy purposes, and she exhibits a balance between work and pleasure with the psychology-related texts and the classic literature titles on the quaint bookcase in the corner. I quietly fold my hands in my lap, aware that she is watching me while she scribbles her findings.

"I haven't felt as depressed," I say. "During some parts of the day, I feel happy, even joyful. Spending time with my daughter always helps my mood. My relationship with Paul is also improving. Our communication has never been better."

"Excellent," she says.

I imagine her notepad with checked boxes in the category of "sane." I love this game.

Mrs. Burke meets my glance. "And your anxiety levels? How has your stress been lately?"

I offer her a sad smile, making sure to appear embattled. Too much instantaneous progress will seem contrived. "I must admit I have been nervous. Still having trouble sleeping. Just restless, I suppose. Too much on my mind. When I can't sleep, I grow anxious. Then, stress follows, which leaves me restless. It's a vicious cycle."

Her pen catalogues my description. "How are you handling this cycle?"

I move my hands to my thighs. "I've been using the deep breathing method you taught me. I picture the tension flowing out of me, from my feet, from my hands, from my head. I find a quiet place, close my eyes, and focus on my breathing."

She smiles. "Wonderful."

Her pen flows across the page. *Check, check, check. I am beating the game.*

"Elaine, I am proud of your progress. What are some steps you can take during this next week to improve your thought process regarding the depression?"

My mind scrolls through its index to find the prepared response. I deliver the speech like a seasoned professional.

"Moving forward, I believe I need to concentrate on living in the moment, maximizing every opportunity, and placing priority on reaching out to others, rather than focusing inward when the depressive feelings arise. I cannot healthily process stress, anxiety, and the cyclical effects of depression if I isolate myself, so I must be committed to connecting with my husband and daughter and keeping the communication lines open. Being honest about what I am feeling is crucial, both to myself and to those I love. Depression affects me, but it does not define me. I will overcome it and find wholeness in who I am and who I want to become."

Mrs. Burke sets the pen down and stares at me, marveling. "Elaine, I have never been so impressed by a patient before. Your self-awareness is exceptional, and I believe you will reach a point very soon where you will no longer need to see me."

With tears welling up, I say, "Thank you, Mrs. Burke. You have no idea how much it means to hear you say that. No idea at all."

***

I arrive back home to find Paul in the kitchen busy reading the newspaper and sipping a glass of amber liquid.

"What did we decide about your drinking?" I say.

He lowers the newspaper and smirks. "It's apple juice, not beer."

I sit down beside him and take his hand. "Sorry. It looked like something else from a distance."

He smiles. "Thanks for checking on me anyway. So, how was therapy?"

"Helpful," I say. I rise and walk toward the stove. "Do you want some dinner?"

"What did you discuss today with Mrs. Burke?" he asks. I can feel him watching me. "Tell me everything, Elaine."

"We discussed my fits of rage, the sleepwalking, and my suicidal thoughts. The focal point today was my despair about my violence against Lisa because of the circumstances of her birth. At the end of our time, Mrs. Burke asked me how I thought I could treat *you* better and make you more aware when the anger is taking hold. I told her I should wake you in the middle of the night every time I feel the hate intensifying, so you can talk me down before I do something rash. She agreed and said that my fear of loss—which relates to my broken childhood, of course—is fueled by a protective instinct. I behave with violence because I am worried that I will lose control by someone else's violence. I want to shield those I love from possible harm, so I am proactive. I expect violence, so I try to prevent it by using violence."

His gazes at me for several moments in awe. "Very interesting. I'm proud of you for making so much progress."

I nod. "Thanks, honey. Your support means everything. I'm ready to be normal again."

"Agreed. I love you," he says. He returns to his newspaper.

"I love you too," I reply.

When he is no longer watching me, I rub my wrists together behind my back. I suppress a smile.

Poor bastard. He doesn't even see it coming.

***

I am backed against the kitchen wall. A horrified Lisa stands at the far corner of the kitchen. Paul stands before me, his hands poised with a thick rope.

"She killed Julia," I say, clenching my fists. "She hurt me. I'm going to hurt her."

"No, Elaine!" yells Paul. "Lisa didn't do anything."

"Mama, please listen to him!" says Lisa.

I sneer at her. "You're a filthy, evil girl."

"Be quiet, Elaine!" Paul implores me.

On the kitchen counter nearby, I see a carving knife, which I snatch and thrust at him. He dodges the blade and knocks the weapon from my hand. It hits the floor with a loud clang. His strong hands shove me against the wall. The snake-like coils of the rope wrap around me forcefully.

"It's for your own good," says Paul.

I glare at him, hate swelling out of control within me.

Lainey, they want to manipulate you and convince you that you're insane. They think you're out of your mind, but they're the ones assaulting a defenseless woman, tying her up like an animal. Who's really insane here? Make them realize how strong you are. Make them pay for this betrayal.

***

My wrists are raw, the flesh peeling and blistered where the rope burns have formed jagged marks across my pale skin. The rope around my chest and arms makes me feel like a caged animal. Paul sits on a wooden chair near our bedroom door, guarding me with watchful intent. I writhe on the bed, trying desperately to loosen the knots.

"Why won't you stop fighting already?" he asks. "It's been three days, Elaine. If you keep struggling, I can't release you."

"I don't deserve this," I say. "You know I am a good person."

He leans forward on the chair, placing his elbows on his knees. "Yes, you are a good person, but you're confused right now."

"What about Lisa? She needs me."

He stiffens. "She's fine right now. She's safe."

I stop struggling with the rope and try another tactic. "Don't you love me, Paul? Why won't you show me how much you love me?"

He swallows hard. "Yes, I love you, Elaine, but—"

"Then kiss me. Untie these ropes. Prove your love for me."

He seems drawn in, momentarily filled with longing, forgetting his awful duty. Then, he flinches, and shakes his head. "No, I can't."

I give him my most heartbroken expression. "Please, don't do this to me. I'm your wife. I'll do whatever you want if you let me go. I won't hurt myself. I won't hurt anyone. I promise."

He sighs and stares at me painfully. "I love you, but I don't believe you."

My expression darkens. He presses his hands to his temples.

"Why did you lie to me?" he asks.

I watch his tears well up. I expect my insides to sting, but I am numb.

"I didn't lie," I say. "I just didn't tell you everything."

"You made it all up, Elaine. You *lied*. You told me you were dealing with your issues in therapy. You're twisted. You described in detail full conversations you supposedly had with Mrs. Burke, but you faked all of it."

I squirm on the bed. "I *did* talk to her about my depression."

He pounds his fist against the door. "That's just a fraction of what's going on, and you know it. Stop lying to Lisa and me. Stop lying to yourself. We can find you the help you need, but if you're going to keep pretending you're fine and putting on this act, then you can't get better."

"You can trust me, Paul," I say. My voice sounds less convincing than I hoped.

He grunts. "The only thing I can trust you to be is untrustworthy."

Lainey, you know he's plotting your ruin, even as he sits in that chair. He only wants to control you, to quench any independence in you. Because he can't be reasoned with, you have to take a different course of action.

"I give up," I say, disheartened. I lie motionless on the bed. "Paul?"

"Yes."

"See how I am behaving now?"

"Yes."

"I've stopped fighting. Now will you untie me?"

"No."

"When will you untie me?"

"When I can trust you."

Thick silence follows. I finally sigh.

"I understand, Paul. I'm sorry. I will be better, I promise. Just give me one more chance. One last chance—that's all I want. We can go to my therapy sessions together. I'll get better. You'll see. I need your help. I need your support. Please don't turn your back on me now." *Give him the clincher. Sell it.* "If I don't improve, I'll have myself committed."

He considers this at length. "Are you lying?"

This time, some of my tears are real. "I hope not."

***

For the past several months, I have been an outer angel living in an inner hell.

Gullible Paul and sweet Lisa have lowered their defenses, assuming I have returned to "sanity." Such a loose term. So elusive. The dark cloud in my mind grows daily. Revenge is a bizarre process, but it must be endured if I am to master and manage my life. I cannot lose control, and I will not allow myself to be hindered by taking responsibility for the consequences of my actions. Those notions are for simpletons like Paul. I live beyond those arbitrary rules.

Currently, they believe I am obedient, docile, and harmless. Supposedly, the therapy has been helping my warped thought processes. Paul thinks he is monitoring my progress and my passivity. Such a well-intentioned yet truly unobservant male—so typical. Even though he never lets me out of his sight, he sees nothing as it truly is.

We attend the weekly therapy sessions, and I give all the "right answers," but not the honest ones. I have been prescribed several pills as a fix for my "issues," but this is only a controlling device, and I will not be controlled. I took the pills in front of Paul for the first few weeks. Now he trusts me to organize my pills and swallow them at the scheduled times. However, they always seem to end up in the toilet, flushed out of sight.

I make my own medication regimen, using the naïve assistance of the local pharmacist. One can easily sneak into a psychiatrist's office at night, swipe a prescription pad, and forge a signature for a patient's prescription. I have a treasure-trove of painkillers, antidepressants, sleep aids, energy uppers, medicines to keep me awake for days on end, and other "cocktails" to fit my ever-evolving moods. I never know which pill I will need, so I am prepared for any situation.

Mrs. Burke, my oblivious therapist, has noted tremendous progress in my temper and outlook on life. All my husband and daughter have seen of me since the tied-up-on-my-bed incident is what they need to see—what I want them to see. Proudly, I present a living snapshot of the person they wish me to be, and it comforts, relieves, and disarms them. Elaine, the poised, glamorous wife has returned, elbowing out Lainey, the unpredictable, twisted alter ego.

Lurking in my mind is a growing shadow, a madness fueled by neither love nor grief, a parasite that knows no rationale or limit. It hounds me to do things I know I should not want to do. I wish I could have shut Lisa up for good, wrap her in a garbage bag, and drop her off on Jeffrey and Christina Hunt's doorstep to become their miracle—the long-awaited daughter they never had. Afterward, I would hug Paul, squeeze the breath out of him, wrap him in a garbage bag, and leave him on our doorstep for the mailman to find.

I wait for the opportunity to exert my power over these feeble creatures who are attached to me like leeches. This will require tact and patience. The family persona is too fragile, too easily shattered, like the wine glass against the rocks. I need to make sure they obey me, while not realizing what they are doing.

That's it, Lainey. Don't lose status, don't lose reputation, don't lose image. Work your magic. Wait and watch. Your time will come. Remember what we need to keep telling ourselves in the meantime.

We are a happy family.
We are a happy family.
We are a happy family.

***

It's May, 1955, and the bombshell has dropped. Lisa is fourteen years old.

"I'm pregnant," she says.

My world numbs as I stare at her in her black baggy clothes. Red acne clusters fight with the brown freckles for dominance of her oily face. The black curls which used to highlight her cuteness now lay in a scraggly, unwashed mess on her scalp. I can smell the pubescent, hormonal aroma coming off her.

My hollow voice asks, "Why?"

She seems prepared for a confrontation. "What do you mean *why?*"

I step further into her bedroom as she steps back, positioning herself between the dresser and the bed.

"Why did you do this to me?" I say.

She steadies herself against the dresser. "It's not about *you*, Mama. There's a boy—"

"I don't want to hear about a boy!" I thunder. "Do you realize what this means for our family? You're only fourteen. How in the hell do you go and get pregnant? How could you do this, Lisa?"

"I'm capable of making my own choices," she says. "I met a boy, and we love each other. That's all there is to it."

"And now you're a whore!" I shout, advancing aggressively until she is within arm's reach.

"Stop it, Mama! I love him. It's Wesley from school. Do you remember? He wants to be a musician. He's sixteen. We've known about the baby for a while. That's why I've been wearing bigger clothes to hide it. I didn't tell you because I knew you'd be upset."

I absorb her words for a moment, noticing her contented expression. Her obvious fulfillment ignites my rage. I rub my wrists together and lean toward her.

"You're going to get rid of it."

She flinches, as if she had predicted what I would say. "No."

"This is not a discussion. You've brought shame on us, and now you're going to make that shame go away."

"I want to have the baby. I want to be with Wesley and raise our baby together."

"Don't try me, Lisa. I don't care about your musician friend who has acted irresponsibly. You are never to see him again. We're going to solve this problem."

"It's not a problem, Mama. It's a baby."

I jab my finger at her. "We have respectability in this city. How could you be so stupid as to ruin what I've earned?"

"I figured you couldn't be more disappointed in me than you already are, so I might as well do what I want. You don't care about me anyway."

"I care about this family," I say, seething.

She snickers. "You care about the *image* of this family!"

Her words paralyze me. I turn away and stare out the window. My wrists continue to rub together.

"You are not going to bring a scandal on our family," I say.

Silence follows, then footsteps, and her hand touches my shoulder.

"Mama?" Her tone exudes longing.

I moan. "What?"

"Why do you hate me?"

In a flash of weakness, my defenses crumble, allowing her to see my pain. "I don't *want* to hate you."

She reaches to grasp my hand, but stops her fingers within an inch of mine. Her physical closeness has the same sensation of disconnect between our mother/daughter bond that has existed for years. I yearn to embrace her, to tell her how sorry I am, and to make right these wrongs. Instead, I stare at her and do not reach out to close the open wound.

"Please, Mama," she says. "Pleasé help me with this. I'm sorry it happened. I didn't plan it. I made a mistake, but please don't make me kill it."

"You can't have a child now," I say. "Not in this house, not with this family."

She bites her lower lip. "I knew you would respond this way, so I've thought of a compromise."

"What kind of compromise?" I say.

She remains calm. "I'll stay in this house, away from the view of your high-society friends. You can hire someone to homeschool me until the baby comes, someone you can pay to keep a secret. Once I deliver the baby, I'll give it up for adoption. I'll do all of that, and I'll even behave better and listen to you, if you promise me something."

My jaw clenches. "Promise you what?"

Her hand touches mine. "Promise me you'll treat me like you love me and want to have a relationship with me."

Her broken expression shatters my heart. Yet, my exterior remains rigid, refusing even to acknowledge the connection she is trying to make.

She's not your daughter, Lainey. Remember what she did. What do you see when you see her face?

Julia's agony resurfaces in my thoughts.

Yes, remember how much you hate her for what she did to Sissy. You can't forgive her, you can't love her, and you can't have a relationship with her. Keep your grudge and the bitterness, or else you'll become weak and you'll forget why you were angry with her.

I withdraw my hand from hers. The ache to stop hating her is strong. I wish we could cherish one another without this poison infecting us, turning us into enemies.

Suddenly, the image of Lisa holding up her newborn baby to the appalling stares and gasping dismay of our high-society friends looms before me.

You can't risk her keeping the baby and shaming you. She will defy you and expose you if you are not savvy in your response. Compromise, Elaine. Give her what she wants for now, and you'll get what you want later. Do what you're best at. Play the part.

"Agreed," I say. "If you will give the baby up for adoption, I promise we can have a new start."

Joyfully, she flings her arms around me and presses her forehead into my neck. I pat her on the shoulder.

Her voice whispers, "Thank you, Mama. Things will be better from now on."

"I know they will," I reply.

Lisa scurries out of the room, almost skipping with excitement.

**

For the past seven months while her foolish mistake has grown in Lisa's womb, I have conducted a trial run of being the kind of mother to her that I always wanted for myself. Unfortunately, in the end, the experiment has failed. Lisa delivered little Cassie on November 12, 1955, the day after her fifteenth birthday. However, the reality has proved too much for me to handle. My baby now has a baby. Something must be done.

***

Soft coos tickle my ears. Lisa sits on the living room couch beside me, wearing a cream tank top and purple sweatpants—the first time I have seen her dress in something other than that unsightly black baggy ensemble in months. Bundled in her arms, with her tiny head cushioned against her mama's shoulder, is Cassie, her eyelashes lifting and falling like a lazy butterfly's wings.

"She's beautiful," I say, smiling.

I run my fingers across the baby's smooth scalp, marveling at the lack of wrinkles and flaws. She knows nothing, fears nothing, and hopes for nothing. She simply breathes and relies on her mother for her needs. This child is blemish free. Even her scent is pure.

"Yes, she is," says Lisa. Her countenance glows, contented and delighted. "I can't believe how much I love her."

I sigh and brush my hand through Lisa's hair as a doting mother would. "I'm glad you love her, but you remember our agreement, don't you?"

"I was hoping maybe—that—well—" Her voice trails off.

Part of me longs to extend compassion, but a greater part considers our high-society circle of friends and their predictable consternation at a child born out of wedlock. I can already hear what they will be thinking to themselves: "If Elaine and Paul cannot control their own daughter, how can they be trusted with our secrets and our money?"

My hand moves to Lisa's shoulder.

"Lisa, dear, think about how this will affect the family. Surely you realize that this baby complicates things for us. Our entire life here could be jeopardized."

Tearfully, she replies. "But I want you to meet Wesley. He wants to be part of Cassie's life, and *I* want to be a part of Cassie's life too. I can't imagine leaving her now. I'm sorry, Mama, but this is too hard for me. Can't I keep her?"

I withdraw my hand. "I don't think that is a good idea."

"Please, Mama—"

"No."

"Why not?"

"Because I don't want you wrecking your life before you've had a chance to live it."

Lisa looks frantic now. "But I can marry Wesley with your permission and then we'll be a family. We'll move away from here if you're worried about your friends finding out. It can be our secret."

I shake my head. "No! You are taking the baby to the orphanage tomorrow and that will be the end of it. I care about you too much to see you struggle with this burden. Believe me, nothing but sadness and difficulty are ahead if you keep this child. I realize it hurts to think about it now, but you'll be grateful to me later. Trust me on this, Lisa. It's best for you."

The tears persist, cascading down her cheeks. She clutches Cassie, as if to protect her from me. Then she abruptly stands up.

"I'm not giving her up, Mama. I won't make her an orphan."

"This is a mistake, Lisa," I say, my tone colder. "Listen to me. You are emotionally attached, and you can't see your situation clearly. You *must* trust me. I'm looking out for your future. I'm not blaming you for what you did. I'm asking you to make it right."

Lisa slips a hand around the baby's head and cuddles it close to her. "This *is* right, Mama. This is what I want. I'm fifteen, and I can take care of her. I know you don't think I'm old enough or mature enough, but I'll figure it out. What I did was wrong, but abandoning her and giving her away would be even worse. Why can't you be loving and caring toward me now, like you have for the past few months? Why are you changing all of the sudden? Can't you see what an impossible position you're putting me in?"

I bolt to my feet and stare down at her. "*You're* the one who's put *me* in this position, Lisa. This is *your* fault, and I'm trying to save you."

"I don't need saving, Mama. I need support."

We glare at each other for a few moments, the tension smoldering.

When I finally speak, my tone is adamant. "I will support you in giving her away for adoption, but nothing more."

Salty water drips down her cheeks. "I hate you," she cries, and with that, she rushes from the room with her daughter.

***

I slip out of bed in the middle of the night. My steps make no sound on the chilly wooden floor. Paul's snores rise and fall as I inch forward, my feet stepping in rhythm with his nasal sounds. Within a few moments, I am at the door. As another snore quakes, I open the door and step into the hallway.

Treading quickly to Lisa's room, I nudge the door ajar and sneak inside. Both she and her child are immersed in dreams. Lisa lies neatly tucked between the bed sheets while the baby lies in her crib nearby. I snatch Cassie from her prison and hurry to the kitchen. All remains quiet and undisturbed in the house.

I slip on my coat and take a final look around to make sure that nothing is out of place. Then I secure the sleeping beauty, leave through the back door, and cut across the grass to the sidewalk. My soft steps creep into my ears. The street is deserted, painted a pale shade of moonlight. Using my free hand, I pull the coat hood down to shield my face and walk as quickly as I can without jostling the baby awake.

This is necessary for your freedom, Lainey. You're helping Lisa. You're helping yourself. This child is a threat to stability. Lisa will understand in time. Trust me.

A few minutes later, I arrive at a massive house set back from the road nearly a hundred yards. A woman waits inside the front gate. As I approach, she extends her arms through a gap between the wrought-iron rods, and I place the slumbering bundle into her hands.

"Her name is Cassie," I whisper. "Take care of her."

The moonlight reveals her tears. "I will. Thank you."

I turn again into the night, not daring to look back.

***

The next morning, as I enter Lisa's room, I see her standing beside the empty crib, staring into the space where her baby should be. She is dressed in black again. Her expression is stoic. Only as I risk a few steps forward does she acknowledge my presence.

"Where did you take her?" she asks.

"Where she belongs," I say.

She folds her arms against her chest as her expression clouds with a mixture of sorrow and anger. "Why, Mama?"

I mirror her posture. "We had an agreement. An agreement *you* offered. Or don't you remember?"

She unfolds her arms and runs her fingers along the edge of the crib. When her hand comes to rest on the wooden support railing, she presses it gently as if smoothing the crown of a baby's head. Pursing her lips, she expels a weighty sigh. "Do you want me to run away?"

"Of course not."

"Then why are you tearing me away from the one thing I love the most?"

"It will be for your good."

Tears glisten on her eyelashes. "So will running away."

I step forward and unfold my arms. "Stop this talk, Lisa. You're free to live your life now. Can't you see what I've done for you?"

Her fingers grasp the crib railing and squeeze it until her knuckles turn white. She glares at me with determination. "I want to see her."

"That's impossible. Forget about her. She's not a part of your life anymore."

Her voice becomes louder. "Where is she? Where did you take her?"

Though my heart aches, I maintain my composure. "She is safe. That's all you need to know."

"Did you take her to an orphanage?"

"She's gone. Let her go," I say, my pitch also rising.

She seems undeterred. "I'm going to get her."

As Lisa attempts to circle around me, I block her path, placing a firm hand on her shoulder. "Don't cross me, Lisa. Leave this alone."

"Don't touch me," she retorts, slapping my hand away.

I raise my fist, and the threat alone causes her to backpedal.

"Will you *please* just leave this alone?" I ask.

She shakes her head. "I'm going to tell Daddy about this."

My hand catches her wrist. "Do you want to drive your father to drink again? Do you want him to be depressed and dejected like he was before? Is that what you want? If so, it will be your fault."

"Let go of my wrist, Mama."

"Not until you promise me you won't tell him."

"You can't stop me from telling him. He will want to know. He loves Cassie, and he wants me to keep her."

I twist her wrist and she cries out. "He doesn't know what he wants, dear, and neither do you. Will you never stop disobeying me and making poor choices? You are a walking tragedy."

She reaches to break my hold on her, but I use my other hand to strike her cheek. Recoiling, she moans and wriggles from my grasp. Before I can restrain her again, she darts around me and out of the room, slamming the door behind her. By the time I reach the bedroom door, I hear the bathroom door down the hallway closing and locking shut.

I try the knob of the bathroom door. It doesn't budge, so I knock gently. Muffled sobs escape from beneath the door.

"You can't hide from me, Lisa. Your father won't be home for lunch for two more hours. I can sit here and wait."

"Leave me alone, Mama. I hate you."

With a sigh, I sit on the floor, resting my forehead against the door. "Lisa, you carried a child for nine months, but you've only been raising her for a week. That's nothing compared to a lifetime of motherhood. You aren't ready for it, and you don't even realize it."

"I'm tired of you controlling my life. I want to make my own choices."

I trace my finger along a groove in the wooden door molding. "Every choice you make leads to trouble. I can't trust you, Lisa. I have to clean up every disaster you cause. How would a new baby be any different?"

"It's not your choice, Mama. It's mine."

"Not any more, dear. Sometimes you have to have choices made *for* you to save you from the bad choices you've made."

No response from the other side of the door. After several seconds, I hear her sit.

"We'll see what happens in two hours," she says.

I smile. "I'm not going anywhere."
Together, separately, we wait.

***

Paul sets his briefcase in the hallway and hurries to my side, his gaze filled with fear.

"What's going on?"

"Mama took Cassie and gave her away," Lisa's voice tattles from the other side of the bathroom door.

"What?" he stammers.

"She doesn't need to be raising a child," I say. "She's too young to make this kind of decision."

He clenches his jaw and glowers at me. Then he focuses on the closed door and his anger morphs into sympathy. "Why don't you come out of the bathroom, Lisa? We'll discuss this together."

"Make Mama promise not to hurt me," whimpers Lisa.

"Of course she won't hurt you, honey," he says, trying to step between me and the door. "I won't let her."

"Don't interfere, Paul," I say, my teeth gritting.

He readies his hand on the door knob. "She's my daughter too, and she's hurting right now. Don't try anything, Elaine."

I lean into him and try to push him away. "This is none of your business."

With his shoulder, he shoves me back. "We're going to bring the baby back."

"Daddy, make her promise not to hurt me," says Lisa, her voice straining.

"I'm not promising anything," I say. "That baby does not belong here!"

"She already hit me, Daddy," her voice whines.

Paul confronts me, forgetting the bathroom door for the moment. "You're not going to touch her again, understand?"

Anger swells within me, fogging my vision. *He's a threat, Lainey. You know what you have to do to keep your world balanced.*

"Get out of my way, Paul. This is the last time I'll tell you."

He crosses the threshold, hooks my arm, and with his strong hand, presses his fingers into my skin.

"Stop this, Elaine, before you get hurt," he says.

Punish him for interfering, Lainey.

With my other arm, I scrape his cheek with my fingernails. Blood wells up in the parallel gashes. He winces but maintains his grip. Enraged, he uses both hands to fling me against the wall. My head burns with pain. I lose my balance and crumple to the floor.

"Daddy, what's happening?!" screams Lisa.

In a blur, I watch Paul dash down the hall, nearly tripping over his briefcase, and race down the stairs.

He's getting the rope from the basement to tie you up and imprison you, Lainey. He wants to dominate you and force you into submission. Don't allow him to escape.

"Daddy, Mama, please stop fighting!" Lisa's voice rings out.

I clumsily struggle to my feet, ignoring the voice behind the bathroom door, and stagger to the stairs. Paul's quick footsteps resonate up the stairwell. Grasping the railing and stumbling down the stairs, I scour the living room, dining room, and kitchen for his figure. Faintly, I hear his footsteps on the basement stairs.

Entering the kitchen, I yank the carving knife from the wooden block next to the stove. The blade is as heavy as a brick in my hand. I hear a door being opened upstairs, as well as footsteps on the basement stairs.

Paul appears in the doorway with the familiar rope in his hands. He takes a determined, cautious step toward me, as I lean against the counter for support. My head continues to throb as the seeping wound drenches my hair.

"Don't make me do this, Elaine," Paul says.

My words return to him garbled, as if they are swimming in an aquarium. "You keep trying to suffocate and control me. I'm tired of you ruling this house. This is *my* family, and I'm not going to let you ruin it."

"Put down the knife," he says.

I advance toward him, using the countertop as a crutch. "You are trying to destroy everything I've worked for." I raise the knife and jab it at him.

He readies the rope, keeping the knife in his sight. "You're not thinking clearly. Please, just set the knife on the counter, and I'll put the rope down."

He's lying, Lainey. You know what he's going to do. He'll bind you and never allow you to be free. He's threatening your independence and stealing your power.

My mood softens, and I lay the knife on the counter. "I'm sorry, Paul. You're right. Please, help me."

He lowers the rope and takes several steps toward me. He still moves cautiously, but he is drawn by compassion and falls into my trap. Before he can extend the rope to imprison me, I snatch the thick carving knife off the counter and plunge it into his chest. I quickly pry the blade loose and stab him again. Then once more for good measure.

In the last moments of his life, Paul stares at me regretfully. He does not seem angry or vengeful, and as he topples onto the kitchen rug, he looks abjectly disappointed. I know I have failed him as a wife, as a friend, and as a companion. As Lisa screams hideously and Paul gasps grotesquely for air, I see only his disillusioned gaze fixed on me. Neither the blood running down the back of my neck nor the blood streaming from his chest matters. The worst wound we have suffered is our mutual awareness that we have allowed our once-happy world to devolve into this nightmare.

His wretched gasping ceases. I turn to Lisa as she sprints across the kitchen.

"You killed him!" she screams.

Dizziness causes me to teeter. "Get some trash bags," I say.

"What?" she asks in shock.

I grip her shoulders. "Go to the garage and bring back some large black trash bags."

She struggles from my grasp and pushes me against the countertop. "You just killed Daddy! Are you insane?"

"No, I'm not insane! Nothing's wrong with me! Now go get those trash bags. We have to take him out and bury him. No one can find out about this. It will destroy us."

"You just murdered him, Mama! You've already destroyed everything!" she bellows.

Her body quakes as she fully grasps what just happened. I quickly rummage through a lower cabinet for the first aid kit. Despite my mental fogginess, I line a gauze pad with strips of medical tape and fasten it to the back of my head over the moist wound. The tape pulls at my hair strands, increasing the throbbing.

"You killed him, you killed him," Lisa repeats to herself, rubbing her wrists together as if they are bound by ropes.

I squeeze her chin. "Shut up! Now listen to me. Unless you want me to hurt you too, you'll do as I say. You're just as guilty as I am."

She tries hard not to stare at the body on the floor. "But I didn't do anything."

I release her chin, wipe blood from the back of my neck, and hold it inches from her. "You did *this* to me." Then I point to the body on the rug. "You did *this* to him. How else can you explain it? If the police come, it's your story against mine. Who do you think they will believe?"

Terror seizes her. "You wouldn't, Mama—"

"Get me some trash bags now!" I scream.

Yes, that's it, Lainey. Fix this problem. Make the mistake go away.

In a daze, Lisa bites her lower lip and hesitates for a moment. When she considers my wild look, she decides against disobeying and hurries to the garage. Once she is out of sight, I press the bandage against my head to secure it. Adrenaline and shock overcome me as I kneel to dislodge the knife from Paul's chest and hide the red-stained blade in the oven.

Plan this carefully, Lainey, and no one will know. Do what is necessary to stay safe.

As Lisa frantically races back into the kitchen, I pause to view Paul for the last time. He is as handsome and distinguished as the day I met him in the bank fifteen years ago. His blue business suit appears dashing on him, in spite of the red blotches. His skin is paler than usual, giving him a vampire-like sheen. I miss him already. His eyes—still open—are not as bloodshot as when he would drink himself to sleep in years past due to the self-proclaimed "stress of living with an unstable woman." Instead, they are glassy, frozen in time, unable to believe that they are lifeless, their last image being a wife's knife coming toward them.

The rustling of trash bags breaks my trance. I turn away, so I do not see his disappointed stare any longer.

***

I walk beside Lisa in the backyard, dragging a red-stained kitchen rug, two shovels, and heavy black trash bags. We enter the dense woods at the rear of the property and maneuver among wiry plants and low-hanging tree limbs. The afternoon breeze comforts my sweaty skin. I watch for signs of intruders invading our privacy and our awful secret. Now, especially, I am grateful that I chose a house far from neighbors.

As we drag the evidence more than fifty yards into the bowels of the forest, my head constantly pulses with pain, but the nagging of responsibility pushes me onward. Lisa and I have not spoken since we began our hauling efforts. Periodically, I have glanced over at her only to find total detachment—a refusal to comprehend what is happening. She remains withdrawn and introspective. Clearly, she perceives this event as unreal, some sort of twisted dream from which she might awaken.

A cloistered cove of fallen branches comes into view behind several thick-trunked trees.

This is the spot, Lainey. Hide it here.

I gesture toward the area, and we pull the rug nearby. We each take a shovel, crouch low, and begin carving out earth from beneath the cove. The dirt proves soft and pliable after last night's rainfall. The sounds are wretched—the slice of the shovel blade as it impacts the earth, the whoosh of the handle as the shovel swings aside, and the final thud of the dirt as it lands on the pile. Within minutes, we have formed a crater almost three feet deep. Perspiration coats our faces, and my scalp wound itches and aches. The scent of blood fills my nose, a foul, coppery odor.

Keep digging. You can't risk wild animals disturbing the grave.

Time passes slowly for the next three feet. Dirt cakes our clothes and skin. We still have not spoken. Lisa's movements have a numbed affectation, her mind obviously trying to disassociate herself from the reality that she is preparing a grave for her father.

After lowering the bloody rug and trash-bag wrapped body into the cavity, we make rapid work of replacing the dirt. Once the task is complete, we return to the house. Lisa gives me a long, chilling stare, then goes up the stairs to her bedroom.

***

In a room laced with shadows, I lie on the bed I once shared with the body now buried in the woods. I view the treasures I will have to leave behind: family portraits framed on the walls, the exquisite black walnut dresser supporting my array of perfumes, the light brown wicker trunk at the foot of the bed which holds Lisa's childhood keepsakes—her first tooth, her first lock of black, curly hair, her first pink baby blanket, and her first pair of shoes. Time to say goodbye to all the firsts we had together.

My hair is slick from my recent shower, and the comfort of my clean white robe enfolds me. My scalp wound is still tender, but the fresh, ointment-soaked bandage and aspirin are helping to minimize the sting. I stare at the ceiling, and images shimmer before me—Aunt Verna being consumed by flames and fury, Julia by grief and anguish, and Paul paralyzed by hurt and disappointment. The visages rise and fall like ghosts, whispering their regrets, wondering about their unfulfilled dreams, waiting for me to join them.

"I'm leaving, Mama," Lisa's voice drifts from the doorway.

I prop up to a sitting position and notice the backpack around her shoulders.

"No," I say, without inflection.

Her body stiffens. "I'm running away and you can't stop me. You've already taken everything from me, so just let me go."

I rise from the bed and open my hands to her. "Lisa, honey, you're not going anywhere alone. Yes, we have to leave now because they will come looking for your father, but you are coming with me. I won't be able to withdraw money from our bank account because your father froze my access to it once I started therapy. I'll never forgive him for that, but I do have some money that we can use to start somewhere else. We'll both miss our friends here, but it's a change we are forced to make. We need to travel together."

She seems perplexed. "You can't be serious?"

I place my hands on my hips and nod. "This is what has to happen. Can't you see that?"

She shakes her head. "You're delusional, Mama. You've lost your mind."

"You don't appreciate the complexity of the situation. We must run and hide. There is no other way. We were both involved in what happened, and there's no way I'm going to allow you to leave on your own."

Her hands ball into fists, and she turns to leave. "Goodbye, Mama. I hate you, and I'm done with you."

"Aren't you forgetting something, Lisa?" My tone teases like an exotic scent.

She regards me with a combination of curiosity and distrust. "What?"

I smile. "You want to see Cassie again, don't you?"

"Don't, Mama, please. Don't hurt her," she gasps.

I smirk. "I'm not going to hurt her. I wouldn't dream of it. She's not mine to hurt. I just thought you might want to know where she is, so you can go to her."

Lisa steps back into the bedroom, forgetting for the moment any thought of fleeing. "Where is she? Tell me, Mama!"

"There, there, my dear," I say, sweeping to her side and placing a consoling arm around her shoulders. "No need to get worked up. I'll tell you, of course, but not yet."

With dread in her voice, she asks, "What do you mean?"

"I'll let you know that secret only if you come with me. Otherwise, I'm afraid I've completely forgotten where I took her."

She brushes my arm from her shoulders and backs away from my outstretched hand. "Mama, how could you do this to me?"

I shrug and smile. "I'm sorry. This is the position your father put us in. He drank too much and became abusive to me. I had to take care of him before he really hurt us. Now we have to find our way, however we can. You're too important for me to let you go. We're bound to each other, and what happened today has to be our secret from now on. Promise me you'll never tell anyone."

"But, Mama—"

"Promise me, or else Cassie will never know her real mother for the rest of her life."

"I promise," she whispers reluctantly.

I lift her chin to meet my gaze. "Good, good, my dear. From now on, our last name is no longer Jeanetta. It's James, and we're never changing it. We're ridding ourselves of our connection to Paul and his weakness. Understood?"

She nods.

I cup her cheek with my hand and wipe away a tear. "That's my girl. Now, go get the knife from inside the oven. We need to take it with us, as a reminder of the freedom we've gained today.

When you come back, you're going to stitch up my wound. No sense traveling with a bloody mess on my head. After that, we're going to pack."

***

The miles flash by in a blur as we ride the bus in silence. Lisa presses her forehead against the window, away from me. We have not spoken since boarding the bus ten hours ago. She has not even looked at me.

Before we left the house, I made a note and attached it to the front door. *We are traveling out of the country unexpectedly for the next year or more. Not sure when we will return. The Jeanettas*

I bought bus tickets to a town called Sleepy Oak, Missouri, only because it was the farthest destination possible from Chattanooga. Our navy blue backpack of belongings lies wedged between our feet. Faint chatter between other passengers drifts into my ears, but I can't afford for it to distract me. Planning our next steps, I need Lisa to see the logic in my actions.

"Are you hungry?" I ask.

Silence. Her gaze remains fixed on the world whizzing by.

"Do you want to talk about what happened?"

Her cheek twitches, but she still offers no words.

"When we arrive in Sleepy Oak, we're going to rent a locker and find the nearest women's shelter to stay for the night. Tomorrow, we'll start fresh."

I tug at her arm, hoping for some kind of response. Her fingers make a fist.

"I know how you feel, Lisa. Believe me, I do. It's just not something I can change." I lower my voice to a whisper. "Your daddy should have known better."

A tear runs down her cheek.

"It was unavoidable," I say. "He wanted power over me. Those who don't have power will do anything to get it, and those who have power will do anything to keep it. Life is cruel, and you have to do what you can to survive. Someday you will understand. Until then, you'll just have to trust me."

We continue to ride in silence.

***

I shiver on the uncomfortable cot. In the darkness, my eyes have adjusted and I can see the outlines of four twin bunk beds and three other cots. A light, female snore ripples from a bunk bed nearby, joined by another heavier one from the other side of the room. Together, they form a discord. The combination of female scents in the room—probably from a collective lack of showering—is slightly nauseating.

The thin blanket provided by one of the workers has been dislodged by my twitching figure. Rolling onto my side, I reach out, expecting to find a lamp on a nightstand, but I grasp empty air.

A cot stirs beside me. Lisa's shadowy figure rolls over to face me. Her voice is a whisper.

"Where is Cassie?"

I listen to the rapid rising and falling of my breath. "Safe. That's all that's important."

She expels a moan. "Why did you take me away from Chattanooga, away from her? I know she's there somewhere."

"Lisa, don't be foolish. She could be anywhere. It won't do you any good to be impatient. I will tell you where she is when I feel our situation is stable and you're ready."

"We're never going to be stable, Mama, you know that. We have no money, you don't have a job, and we don't even have a place to live."

"I'm working on that, dear. Hush now."

"What do you mean you're working on that?"

"Quiet, Lisa. The sooner you do what I say, the sooner you'll see Cassie."

She responds with silence.

In the darkness, as seconds turn into minutes and I still cannot sleep, tears well up. I miss Paul. I wish he had not crossed me. I miss Lisa. I wish she didn't despise me and love her child more than she loves me. I miss myself too. I wish I could cut through my brain fog and not worry about my sanity. I know I can't reveal these struggles to my daughter. They will justify her anger and her desire to run away and leave me alone. I must keep her close and confined for both her protection and mine. She is my only source of sanity, and I cannot part with my one remaining hope to have what I want in this life.

"I'm sorry for everything, Lisa," I whisper into the darkness. "I didn't want it to be this way. I hope you'll be able to forgive me someday."

She responds with deepening silence. After a few moments, she rolls over and turns her back to me. I bury my wet face in the thin pillow.

***

The next morning, I push open a bathroom door to find Lisa watching me with skepticism.

"Do you really think this is going to work, Mama?"

"It has to," I say.

After glancing around to ensure we are alone, I step into the narrow, dank locker room and place our navy blue backpack in storage locker 205. The tip of a sharp object in the backpack presses against the cloth material and catches my finger. Lisa locks the compartment and shoves the key into her pocket.

I wait until she is watching me to ask, "So, how do I look?"

"Nice enough, I guess," she says, with no expression.

"Is the perfume strong enough?"

"Yes, Mama. Strong enough to make me gag."

I smooth out the wrinkles on the frilly yellow dress, arrange my hair, turn my back toward her, and point to my bandage-free scalp.

"Do the stitches still look clean?"

"Yes."

"You can't see them at all?"

She groans. "No, you can't see them."

I turn to her. "Watch your tone, dear. It's unbecoming."

"I don't like this plan," she says. "Can't you just tell me where Cassie is? I'll leave you alone, and I'll never tell anyone what happened. Please, Mama, I promise—"

"No," I say.

She bites her lower lip. "I miss Daddy. I miss his voice, his face—"

"Not another word, understood? Unless you want to live on the street and beg for the rest of your life, stop talking about him and start helping me. I hate this situation as much as you do. He's gone. I can't fix that. What I *can* do is try to give us stability again. We need to be provided for, and that means I need to find a husband quickly. Now, quit complaining, and do your job."

She sighs and stares at her shoes. "Yes, Mama."

"Good. So, once more, how many dresses?"

"Three."

"What colors?"

"Blue, green, and red."

"Yes, yes. Which stores?"

"The boutique on the corner, the department store two streets over, and the small shop next to the Italian restaurant."

"Very good. What do you say if you're caught?"

"That my mother told me she paid for the dress and we need to find her to sort out the issue."

"And then?"

"I start to cry, point to a woman as far away as possible, and then run away with the dress when the person goes to get her."

"Excellent. I'll meet you here in four hours. That should give both of us plenty of time."

I wait for her to acknowledge me, but she maintains her inordinate fascination with the floor. I place my hands on her shoulders.

"Just remember, dear. The sooner this is over, the sooner you'll get to see your daughter."

Finally, she looks at me, unable to conceal her longing. I respond with a satisfied smile.

***

I am standing in the entryway of an elegant restaurant, marveling at the décor—high back wooden chairs with flower patterns carved into the top rails and legs, bell lamps adorned with tear drop designs, and a series of curvy mirrors displayed on the walls. An ornate chandelier embellishes the main room, and delicious scents waft from the kitchen. My stomach growls with hunger. Couples dressed in finery are seated at polished tables, their lively chatter filling my ears. I take a deep breath and steady myself. A tuxedoed host steps to meet me.

"Will you be dining with us this afternoon, Miss?"

I scan the scene, spotting a man with graying hair sitting alone at the far corner of the room. He appears to be older than I. His black suit is dapper, his slightly graying hair is perfectly parted, and his gold watch sparkles from the light of the chandelier.

"Yes, thank you," I say. "Would you mind seating me with that gentleman over there?" I point to the loner. "I'm here to see him. It's a surprise visit. I am a close friend of a business acquaintance of his, so we've never met. I was told to meet him here to deliver a message."

The host nods. "Of course, Miss. Please, follow me."

I weave between the tables behind the host. None of the high-class patrons considers me to be out of place as I pass by. I am obviously another well-to-do, respectable woman on a lunch break.

We arrive at the man's table. He does not seem to notice us at first, his gaze being focused on a newspaper on the tabletop. A quick check confirms a ring-less fourth finger. The host folds his hands at his waist and smiles.

"Mr. Taylor, there is a lady here who wishes to speak with you. She says she was sent to deliver a message."

The man glances up with surprise, mixed with interest. His features are plain—tired almond eyes, drooping cheeks, and a wrinkled brow—but all I fixate on is his expensive watch and suit. He pushes back his chair and stands.

"Yes—if you please," he says, his voice sturdy and polite.

The host pulls out the opposite chair from the table and motions for me to be seated. I willingly follow his instruction. The elderly man waits for me to sit until seating himself again.

"Your server will be with you shortly. Enjoy your meal," the host says, before dissolving back to the restaurant entrance.

We exchange glances. He seems taken aback by my intrusion, so I offer a coy smile.

"I apologize for interrupting your lunch, sir."

"I don't understand, Miss—"

"Elaine James," I say. "I'm pleased to meet you, Mr.—"

"Ernie Taylor," he says.

He extends his hand across the table to shake mine with practiced poise.

"Have we met before, Ms. James?"

"I'm afraid not. Surely I would have remembered such a handsome man."

A blush rises in his cheeks. "I must correct you, Ms. James. Of the two of us, I think it is *you* who would be the memorable one."

"You are *too* kind," I say, lowering my gaze as if embarrassed.

He smiles. "So, to what do I owe this unexpected meeting?"

I give him my most alluring expression. "Actually, Mr. Taylor, our meeting is under false pretenses. I informed the host that I was a friend of a business acquaintance of yours. To be frank, because I do not know you, I certainly do not know any of your business acquaintances. The truth is that when I walked into the restaurant, I saw you, and something compelled me to meet you. I am sorry for the unconventional introduction."

He seems awed by my explanation. "So, you simply picked me out of the crowd and wanted to have lunch with me?"

I nod. "Yes, Mr. Taylor. As odd as it sounds, something tells me it's right. I am new to Sleepy Oak, and I have not made any friends yet. I don't mean to sound forward, but once you caught my eye, I couldn't look anywhere else. I have a flair for adventure, so I thought getting to know you would be worth the intrigue."

By now, he is mesmerized. "Well, Ms. James, you seem delightful, and I am both flattered and charmed. May I buy you lunch?"

I flash another coy smile. "That would be wonderful, but I certainly don't want to impose on your time."

He chuckles. "Ms. James, miracles don't often happen to businessmen like me, so please let me indulge this one while it is happening."

I laugh and slide my hand across the table to touch his. "I was right about you, Mr. Taylor. You *are* worth the intrigue."

He blushes and grins. "Please, call me Ernie."

"Only if you call me Elaine."

We gaze at each other affectionately.

"All right, Elaine," he says, entranced. "It would be my pleasure to dine with you."

I am dazzled by his expensive watch and finely pressed suit.

"So, Ernie, after we eat lunch, would you mind showing me around this quiet little town?"

With boyish excitement, he replies. "I'd love to."

***

I perch at the window of the master bedroom on the fifth floor of the stately mansion, reflecting on the past year and a half since I arrived in Sleepy Oak, Missouri.

Three more dates and three different dresses is all it took for Ernie Taylor to fall in love with me. I admire his time management in that respect. We met at the restaurant on November 21, 1955, he proposed to me during a carriage ride in downtown Sleepy Oak on December 7, 1955, and we were married in a low-key City Hall ceremony on December 21, 1955. I introduced Ernie to Lisa the day after we became engaged. He took to her surprisingly well, considering he was a fifty-five-year-old wealthy bachelor without the prospect of either a wife or a child. The money from his oil business easily persuaded several construction companies to work together around the clock to erect a five-story, thirty-one-room mansion "wedding present" in record time, even in the middle of winter. The blueprints were completed the day of our engagement, and the house was finished on December 31. We moved in on the first day of the new year.

All Ernie has wanted has been a companion, and all I have wanted is the lifestyle that being his companion provides. With this unspoken understanding, we have lived in two different worlds within the same house. We hired a butler/gardener, Harold, and a cook/housekeeper, Marlene. Lisa opted for a room on the third floor, two floors below our master bedroom.

I immediately gathered miscellaneous items for each room of the house. I called them "distinct character" items because each one represented a dream I'd had while growing up—a dream that could never be fulfilled at the time. These objects are, in a sense, characters from the story I always wanted for my life—places I wanted to visit, finery I wished I had, and gifts I wished I could lavish on loved ones. Each item is uniquely special to me, though no one else can understand its meaning: a rug from Peru, a miniature Eiffel Tower, ornate china dishes, a vintage gramophone, countryside paintings, a framed photograph of twin girls playing in the park, and a chess set, among many others.

I have loved the chess set most of all. It is a "distinct character" collectible that I dream of, not in the past, but in the present, hoping to use it as a way to spend time with Lisa to repair our fractured relationship. Lisa played chess with me for the first few months, but she stomped off one day, saying that she wanted nothing to do with me. Since then, the game playing has ceased. However, I cannot bring myself to discard the set because even though I have promised myself never to touch it again, it represents that small space between the two conflicting emotions of love and hate that I feel for her—that tiny ray of hope that things might someday change between us.

Lisa and I have been eternally at war within the walls of this massive house, chasing each other around in our mutual misery. My kind, naïve husband accepts the conflict, though he doesn't understand it. He is a wonderful, aloof benefactor, the perfect man to underwrite the lifestyle in which I flourish. I don't have the time or energy to deal with a man who resists me with strong opinions and chauvinism. Ernie remains a background player, a piece of scenery on the stage, while my spotlight remains on Lisa. She has been bitter and reclusive since both her child and father disappeared. Only when Ernie travels on business, does she draw closer to me, but only to either dredge up the past or pester me about the future.

I long to fill in the blanks of her life, those secrets of my past that I know eat away at her. Yet I cannot risk the pain that would accompany such honesty. Perhaps someday we can find a way to make amends. For now, we must creep around among the shadows, escaping each other's heart, hiding our hurt behind our hate.

***

As I stand in Lisa's room, I glance around in disappointment at the bookcase filled with pop culture magazines instead of classic literature titles, the cherry wood desk covered with her gothic sketches of ghosts, goblins, vampires, and other such hideous, unladylike creatures, and the piles of unwashed clothes forming a knee-deep trail between her bed and the closet. I bristle at the sound of the voice bellowing behind me.

"I'm sixteen, Mama. It's time to let me go. Tell me where she is!"

I stare at the white wall. "We should paint your bedroom walls. That way, maybe you'll have a change of attitude and learn to appreciate what you have."

"You're talking nonsense," she says, tugging on my shirtsleeve. "I'm going crazy in this place. I need to leave."

I refuse to look at her. "You belong here. Perhaps pink would be a good color for these walls? What do you think?"

She steps in front of me and forces me to see her. "Mama, this isn't right, our being here. You're married to a man you don't even love. We're taking advantage of his money just so we can feel stable. I miss Daddy. I wish things could go back to the way they were."

I stiffen. "Don't talk about him again. This is your home now. Stop being ungrateful for what we've gotten. To survive, you have to take what you can in this life. Life is cruel, remember? You just have to get used to it. Quit being weak."

Her expression is steely. "Where's my daughter, Mama? I've done everything you've asked for a year and a half. Where is she?!"

"Promise me you'll stay, and then I'll tell you."

This statement obviously bewilders her. "What? You *told* me I could go to her once we were in a stable situation. Now you want me to stay? How can I reach her if I'm stuck here?"

I rub my wrists together, chaffing the skin. "You have to finish high school."

"I don't care about school. I need to find my daughter."

I cross my arms. "You are safe here. You have everything you need. Why are you still worrying about that child?"

"Because she's mine! Cassie is *my* baby, not some stranger's. Tell me where I can find her."

"I'm afraid I can't do that," I say, calmly.

"Why are you doing this to me, Mama?"

I cup her chin. "Just like before, it's *you* who's putting me in this position."

She raises her hands in exasperation. "You've never done anything but hate me."

"Don't break my heart more than it already has been, Lisa."

I release her chin and step away from her.

Her voice is hoarse with emotion. "What have I done to make you hate me so much?"

I run my fingers across the wall while avoiding her stare. "As I told you before, dear, I've never *wanted* to hate you. It's something that was forced on me. Just like the darkness in our minds, it's something I can't purge. I know you've felt it too, that unstable feeling."

She cautiously steps closer. "What are you saying?"

I continue to trace the imperfections in the wall with my finger. "It's like a poison in your thoughts. The desire of one part of your mind to do something that horrifies the other part. That's how it is for me. My hatred of you and my love for you are equal. Sometimes I can resist the dark thoughts. Other times, they consume me. You understand, don't you?"

She sighs audibly. "Please, just tell me where Cassie is."

"Lisa, admit to me that you've had the same kind of thoughts."

A tentative pause follows. Then she places her hand over mine and presses it to the wall. "Yes, I've had those thoughts. They're like a confusing fog that I get lost in. But I don't want to give in to it. I want to find a way to stop it from happening. I need to get to my daughter. You can't control me anymore, Mama. I'm going to leave and create something just for *me*. Please act like a real mother for once and treat me like I'm a daughter you care about."

She lifts her hand and allows me to walk away to think about her words.

"You don't want pink walls then?" I ask.

"No, Mama. I don't want walls of any color *here*."

"If I tell you where she is, will I ever see you again?"

A weighty pause follows. "I promise I'll come back," she says. "I don't know when, but I'll come back."

"And you want to leave now?"

"Yes."

"How do you plan to get Cassie back?"

"Wherever she is, I'm going to find a way. This is something I want to do alone. Please don't interfere. Just tell me where she is, and the rest will be up to me."

I consider for a moment. "What about everything else that's happened?"

"I'll never say a word about it to anyone, I swear. I'll keep your secrets. You can stay here and have the life you want, and I will go and find the life I want. Do we have a deal, Mama?"

I feel my carefully controlled world losing its equilibrium. Seeing Lisa with such resolve, I cannot help but feel proud of her. I tried to make her strong, but she honed this indomitable will on her own. She will survive. I can see it. I need her more than she needs me now, and even though it wrenches my heart, I must let her go. Either I release her now, or I will end up being the object of her pent-up wrath.

"Yes," I say softly.

"You promise?"

"I promise."

To my surprise, she throws her arms around me.

"Thank you," she whispers in my ear. "Please don't lie to me."

"I won't—this time. I'm sorry. I *do* love you, Lisa."

Without a reply, she squeezes me tighter.

***

This will be the final entry in my journal. It is too painful to continue.

I have spent three months transcribing my story on these pages, hoping to clear the fog in my brain, but the darkness has only thickened around me. My mind is slipping away. I've discovered that sanity is like sleepwalking—you don't know you're experiencing it until one day you wake up and it's gone.

My heart has been broken, and my depression is like a cancer poisoning me. My sweet daughter will never see me as her mother. Once she learns the truth, I will have ruined the possibility of any relationship with her, and all my threats and commands will be meaningless. Ironically, I am too shattered to hide my past from her any longer. It is time for her to know everything. I will make this diary available to her and accept the consequences.

She is leaving, and I am alone. It is what I deserve.

Elaine James

July 19, 1957

Lisa James

May 30, 1960

Cindy, my sweet baby, this is Mama. I am adding this part of my story to the end of your Grandma Elaine's journal because I know you will read it someday, and I want you to know what happened. As I am writing this, you are asleep in your crib, perhaps dreaming of a better life than the one I am able to give you. Whenever you read this, please know that I love you and I will always be proud of you, no matter what.

No doubt, many things you have read here have frightened you and might make you think less of your Grandma Elaine and me. We are not a perfect family, or even a healthy one, but it's what we were born into and it's what you've been born into as well, so the only thing we can do now is try to change what happens from this point on.

How many nights I cried myself to sleep after I found out that Elaine was not my real mother, and that her sister Julia died giving birth to me. I cried because I never had a chance to know my mother and I missed that, and I cried because the only mother I had known was kept from loving me by the hatred she felt toward me. I don't want to relive the past. What's done is done, and it's time to move on. You need to know what happened after I was given Grandma Elaine's diary and boarded a bus to Chattanooga to find Cassie.

Your Grandma Elaine had arranged for me to rent a small apartment, and she had given me enough money to live on for a time. When I arrived in Chattanooga, I didn't visit our old house because it would have been too painful.

It took me a week to gather enough courage to go to the Hunt family to try to find my baby.

***

I stand before a front gate surrounding a regal estate, hoping my cute pink dress will showcase my innocence and aid my cause. Swallowing the lump in my throat, I press the intercom button. As I wait, I admire the well-groomed lawn fronting the lavish three-story house. My reverie is interrupted by a voice.

"Who's there?" a woman asks through the speaker.

I rub my wrists together. "My name is—Lisa James. I'm the daughter of—"

"Elaine, yes, I know," says the woman. "What do you want?"

"Is that you, Mrs. Hunt?"

A lengthy pause. "What do you want?"

I focus on the security camera next to the speaker box. "I was wondering if I could see Cassie?"

An even longer pause. "Where are your mother and father? When you did get back from your travels abroad?"

I hide my hands behind my back and dig at my fingernails. "We actually had to move away unexpectedly. They're not coming back. I just came back for a short time. My mama told me about what happened to the baby—*my* baby. I was hoping I could see Cassie and take her with me. I'm ready to raise her now."

"Please go away. It would be best if you never came back here. If you stay by the gate, I'll have to call the police. I'm sorry. Goodbye."

The intercom clicks off. I stand, immobile. Finally, I head down the sidewalk toward my lonely apartment.

***

I hide behind a patch of bushes, trembling. The sun beams like a radioactive orange high in the sky. Perspiration coats my body, giving off an unfavorable aroma. The tall, thick greenery bristles against my skin, but I am concentrating on something else—the family picnicking on the grass in the park fifty feet away.

An elegant, refined couple, both middle-aged, sits on a blanket with a baby who appears to be about a year and a half old. Nearby, a gray-haired woman, possibly the nanny, unpacks lunch from a basket and sets out paper plates. The man and woman are enthralled with the child. The toddler smiles, giggles, and crawls across the blanket. As I watch her, tears roll down my cheeks and splash onto my rubbing wrists.

"Come to me, Cassie," says the woman, patting the blanket. "Walk to mama."

My baby slowly stands, stumbles a few steps, and then lunges forward, as the woman scoops her up into her arms. She kisses Cassie's face and neck. The baby screams with delight, and the man grins from ear to ear. Even the nanny smiles and joins in the laughter.

"She is always so happy," says the nanny.

The woman nods. "That's because she's so loved."

"Indeed, Mrs. Hunt. It's wonderful that you finally have the daughter you've always wanted."

The woman beams, patting the baby's back. "I've never been happier in my life. How is lunch coming along, Nancy?"

"Almost ready, Mrs. Hunt," says the nanny. "We're having turkey club sandwiches, potato salad, freshly picked strawberries, and chocolate cream pie for dessert."

"Sounds delicious," says Mr. Hunt.

"I can hardly wait," says Mrs. Hunt. "This is a perfect way to say 'goodbye.'"

Nancy glows with pride. "I'm glad you approve of the menu. I'm also glad you trust me to watch Cassie while you are on vacation next week."

"Of course," says Mrs. Hunt. "You're like a grandma to her."

The adults turn their attention to lunch while continuing their carefree banter. Unnoticed by the grownups, Cassie watches the woods fifty feet away, where she sees a hand waving at her. She gurgles in amusement, but no one notices—no one except her real mother. For a brief moment, I feel a strange sensation—hope.

***

I sit in a booth at McDonald's, munching on French fries. Boisterous chatter fills the air, and children pull their mothers by the hand, pointing at this, asking for that. The kid's play area bustles with sugar-fueled activity—yelling, leaping, and screaming. I focus on the gray-haired woman seated with her back to me in the next booth. Beside her, my child stands on the booth seat, wearing a chocolate-stained *I Love Mommy* bib and hopping joyfully.

I watch as Nancy encircles her arms around Cassie, allowing her to bounce safely. The beautiful baby girl turns in my direction. She sees my waving hand and smiles even wider. She points at me and jabbers incoherently. Nancy half-turns in her seat and smiles at me.

"I think she likes you," she says.

My breath catches. "I like her too."

Cassie claps her hands and bubbles with glee.

"She's such a happy little thing," says Nancy.

I nod. "What's her name?"

"Cassie."

I fight to keep my composure. "That's a beautiful name. Her mother must be very proud. I know *I* would be."

Cassie leans against the seatback and reaches for me with both arms.

"Cassie normally doesn't take well to strangers, but she seems right at home with you. Why don't you come and sit with us, unless you have somewhere else to go?"

My heart pounds. "I'd love to. Thank you."

I leave my food and sit across from them. Cassie wiggles and tries to crawl onto the table. Nancy laughs and moves a cup of chocolate ice cream out of the way.

"She's certainly determined to get to you. What's your name?"

"Lisa," I reply.

This child, who continues to reach for me, totally enraptures me.

"I'm Nancy. Nice to meet you. I'm her nanny. Would you like to hold her?"

"More than anything," I whisper.

Trembling, I wrap my arms around Cassie and bring her close to me. "Hi, baby." Her features are exquisite—bright, innocent eyes and fair, unblemished skin. "You're precious," I coo softly.

Cassie smiles, and my heart skips several beats. She curls her fingers around mine and nuzzles my cheek. I tenderly kiss her forehead.

"She really seems to like you," Nancy says.

My surroundings seem to disappear. Only Cassie and I, holding each other, transferring back and forth the love we have never been able to share, exist at that moment. The tears I have suppressed up to now fall freely.

"Are you all right?" asks Nancy.

I sniffle. "I'm fine. I'm sorry. I had a baby once, and I lost her. She just reminds me of—never mind—I'm sorry."

"Do you need me to take her back? Is this too hard for you?" she asks.

I clutch Cassie to me. "No, please, just let me hold her a little longer. I miss her. I mean—I miss *my* baby—the one she reminds me of."

I hesitantly look toward Nancy. Suddenly, my defenses collapse and I feel completely vulnerable. Nancy sees my reaction and the color fades from her cheeks.

"What did you say your name was?" she asks.

Cassie is resting contentedly on my shoulder. My voice sounds far away. "Lisa."

Nancy leans forward. "What's your last name?"

"Why?" I ask, biting my lip.

"I only began working for the Hunts after Cassie came into their family a year and a half ago, so I don't know you, but you seem to know Cassie already and feel connected to her. Cassie is an adopted baby. What's your last name, Lisa?"

"James," I whisper.

She gawks. "*You're* Lisa James?"

"Yes."

"Mrs. Hunt, her mother, warned me not to allow you near the house or the baby while they were gone. Why did she tell me that?"

My grip on Cassie tightens. "Because I'm Cassie's real mother. She's my baby. My mother, Elaine, gave her to Mrs. Hunt right after she was born. My family moved away, but I've come back to get her. Please, don't take her away from me again."

Nancy scratches her fingernail on the tabletop. "You're her real mother?"

I nod.

Her expression turns to disbelief. "Are you sure?"

I smile. "I know my own daughter."

"I'm not sure I can believe all of this," she says, as if to herself.

"Where did Mrs. Hunt say the baby came from?"

"An orphanage out of state."

I shrug. "Well, she actually came from ten minutes down the street. My mother took her without my permission and gave her away. You have to believe me."

She squints at me, trying to discern the truth. "Please give Cassie back to me," she says, extending her arms.

I plead with her. "I'm begging you, don't take her away. I need her."

"I need to leave," says Nancy. "Hand her over, please."

My heart plummets, as I loosen Cassie's hold on me, kiss her forehead once more, and reluctantly surrender her. Before Nancy can slide out of the seat, I reach to catch her hand.

"If you won't let me have her, please at least let me see her once in a while. I promise I won't interfere with her life. I just want to be around her and know she's cared for."

"I don't know—" says Nancy.

I'm bordering on panic at this point. "I'm desperate. She's all I have, and I lost her. If she was *your* daughter, what would you do?"

She pauses, then views me with compassion at the sight of my free-falling tears.

"I would probably do what you're doing," she says.

I squeeze her hand. "Thank you."

As she turns to leave, Nancy tries to reassure me. "Lisa, I don't know that I should trust you, but somehow I believe you. Cassie does look like you, after all. You realize that I can't give her to you, and you can imagine how much trouble I'll be in if I bring up the issue with Mrs. Hunt. So it has to be our secret. This is what I'm going to do. I travel into town by myself every week to pick up groceries and supplies for the house. From now on, I'm going to bring Cassie with me, and we can meet you."

I smile broadly. "Nancy, I can't tell you what this means to me."

"Do you have any money?" she asks.

"No."

"And I don't suppose you have a job yet either?"

I cringe. "No."

She pats my hand. "I know the manager here, so I'll put in a good word for you. You should apply immediately. This can be our meeting place, and I will bring Cassie once a week during your lunch break. Just remember, if Mrs. Hunt finds out, you will probably never see your daughter again, so be very careful where you go and what you do in town."

"I understand," I say, "and I'm more grateful than you'll ever know."

She nods. With her free hand, she rummages through her purse and sets several twenty-dollar bills on the table. "Take this. It's not much, but it will get you started. Take care of yourself, and I will see you soon."

I grasp her hand once more. "Thank you again."

With that, Nancy turns to leave.

***

Cindy, can you imagine how just a single ray of hope can affect a woman who has lived in shadows her whole life?

By the next week, I had a job at McDonald's. As we had planned, once a week Nancy brought Cassie to see me during my lunch break. This became the happiest half hour of my life every week. I always brought fries and a burger for myself and chocolate ice cream in a cup for my baby girl. We sat at the same corner table, perfectly at home in the midst of other families having lunch together. Nancy and I became good friends. I lived for every Tuesday afternoon when "Grandma" Nancy would bring little Cassie to see her mama at work. It was my sacred half hour of heaven.

One day, I asked Nancy to take a picture of Cassie for me. That's the picture I want you to see someday, so you can know you have a sister. I'll get it to you somehow. In case I never get a chance to bring Cassie home to be a part of our family, I want you to understand how much I care for her, just as I care for you.

Four months passed, and on the first Tuesday of December in 1957, Nancy failed to appear with Cassie. I sat at our regular booth, waiting, watching the clock for thirty minutes. By the end of my lunch break, I had to return to work. I tried to hide my disappointment as I resumed my shift at the cash register.

Every Tuesday after that, I sat at our regular booth and waited, but they never came again. Nancy did not contact me to explain what was wrong. I had no idea why I wasn't able to see my baby. Without other options, I continued to work at McDonald's, working hard for a small paycheck, hoping every Tuesday that I would see Nancy and Cassie, but that never happened. I never saw Cassie again.

As the weeks turned into months, I experienced a deep depression. The ache to see my daughter was so great that I started to think what it would be like to have another baby to love. In my apartment, I cried myself to sleep after work and woke up red-eyed in the morning before my next shift. The urge to be the kind of mother I wanted to be—one who was actually with her child— was so strong that I accepted a date with the first man who flirted with me at the cash register.

His name was Curtis Young, and he's your daddy, Cindy. He was twenty years old when I met him in November, 1958, just after I had turned eighteen. You have to understand how lonely and desperate I was to feel something, anything at all. Against my better judgment, I let him take me to his beat up shack after our first date, and I never left. We lived together starting in 1959. Several times I went to the Hunt house and tried to make contact, but no one answered the intercom. I had been cut off completely.

One day, after your daddy and I had been together for six months or so, I told him I wanted to have a baby. He laughed at me and told me that was the stupidest idea he'd ever heard. I told him I was eighteen and could handle the responsibility, but he said he didn't want to have kids anytime soon. I was heartbroken. I told him if he didn't want to have a child, then I couldn't stay with him. He said he would only think about having a baby with me if we were married because then I wouldn't be able to leave him with a baby to take care of. It sounded selfish to me, but I was hurting and desperate. I tried to convince him to propose to me. He was reluctant at first, but eventually he gave in.

Curtis proposed to me in July, 1959, and we were married in the same month. I convinced him to try to have a child, and by the first week of August, I was pregnant. You were born on May 2, 1960, and I was finally happy.

Your daddy currently works at a lumberyard, and he treats me well enough, I suppose. However, he's grown more irritable since you were born. The nice man I first met at the McDonald's cash register is long gone, and he's not coming back, so I have to keep quiet to avoid his rage. I just hope his yelling doesn't turn into something more violent down the road. He hates his job, he hates Chattanooga, and he hates our house, but we're stuck here, barely able to make our bills each month. I keep quiet whenever I get upset about his behavior because I worry about how he will react. Even though he's grown tired of me, as long as he treats you well while you grow up, I'll get along okay. I don't think he'd ever be mean enough to hit me. I hope I'm right about that.

Your daddy knows nothing about Cassie or anything else of my family, and I prefer to keep it that way. I don't trust him to know my past. I've become very good at lying or "inventing" my story. I suppose recreating a dreamy life for yourself is easier than remembering the one you've actually lived.

I sent postcards to your Grandma Elaine after I married your daddy and after you were born, but I didn't want her coming to Chattanooga to be a part of my life again. I couldn't risk her influencing you. She's a dangerous, unstable woman, as I'm sure you've realized after reading her journal. Right now, my life with you here is fragile, and it's not something she can be involved in. Bad things accompany her, like a sickness that never goes away. I don't want you to be infected.

So, that completes the part of the story you didn't know. I'm going to bury this journal under our house, so your daddy doesn't find it. I hope you discover it someday, and I hope it gives you what you need to know so you can put the pieces together. I don't know how old you'll be by the time you read these pages, but I want you to remember how much I love you and that I'll always be proud of you. You're my angel, and I only want the best for you. You and Cassie are so much alike, and I hope you get the chance to know her. Please find a way to save your sister, if she is still missing by the time you find this journal. Lead her back to us, Cindy. Bring her home and reunite our family.

Love always,
Mama

PART THREE:
Awakening

Cindy James

I bolt awake, my chest aching, my throat raw, as if I have been crying for days. A loud screaming noise permeates the air, and I quickly realize it is coming from me. I feel a constricting pressure on my shoulders.

"Cindy!" Tony shouts.

I see his panicked expression. Lexi stands near, also filled with anxiety.

My screaming stops, as I try to get my bearings.

"What happened?" I ask.

Tony's intense grip on my shoulders lessens. "You were dreaming."

My lungs feel wafer thin, unable to lift enough air to speak. "I—I—was there—"

"Where?" he asks.

My heart pulses like an automatic weapon. "It was just like—their stories—"

Lexi stares at me. "Whose stories, Mama? What did you dream?"

I struggle to sit, leaning against the headboard. "Elaine and Lisa," my voice sputters. "I dreamed I was *them*. Everything we read in the journal, I was living in my dream. I was there, first as my Grandma Elaine and then as my mama, living in their bodies, living their past lives."

Tony purses his lips. "I don't know that coming here was the best idea. Maybe we should go back home."

I grow stern. "No, we have to find Cassie. We have to save her."

"Do you think she's still here in Chattanooga?" asks Lexi.

My voice is determined. "She has to be."

Lexi and I stare intensely at each other. The urgency is palpable.

Tony, however, seems reticent. "This is going to be dangerous."

I swing my legs over the side of the bed, simmering inside. "I want to know my sister."

Lexi nods. "And I want to know my aunt."

Tony smiles wryly. "I thought you'd say that. So, how about some breakfast and then we try to find our missing family member?"

Neither Lexi nor I can hide our enthusiasm.

"We'll have to shower first," I say.

"That will give me plenty of time to keep researching," he says.

I circle around the bed and spot his open laptop on the couch. "Researching what?"

He flashes his trademark grin. "I think I've found her."

"What?" I stammer.

"Where?" says Lexi.

He motions toward his laptop. "She's here in Chattanooga, and she's married to Victor Flinder. Victor is now mayor of the city, just like his father Sam was. I assumed that the Hunt family might have tried to marry her off to Victor. So I did a search on Cassie Flinder, and her name came up immediately. There are pictures of them at high-class functions—dinners, fundraisers, political events, the works. She now goes by 'Cassandra.' Her maiden name was Hunt. I'm positive it's her."

I bolt to the couch, plopping down to stare at the computer screen. My body is drawn instinctively toward the image. Lexi joins me.

"That's her," I say, excitedly. "That's my sister, Cassie."

A photo of a middle-aged man and woman in formal attire is posted with the caption: *Mayor Victor Flinder's campaign for state governor boosted by extravagant dinner party for political who's-who.* The man has finely groomed black hair, a handsome profile, and a politician's shark-like grin. The woman is tall, slender, and gorgeous, and her chic haircut brands her as a woman of class. The black scarf around her neck complements her stunning red dress. She exudes authority and poise.

"It's definitely her," I repeat.

The three of us stare in wonder, absorbing the magnitude of the moment. Then Tony rubs his hands together like a mischievous child.

"So, do you want to go see her?"

Lexi and I exchange gazes.

"How fast can you get ready, Lexi?" I ask.

She grins. "As fast as you can, Mama."

Lexi James

The car stops before an iron gated four-story home. The silver mailbox quietly announces *The Flinders*. Even from the backseat, I can see two security cameras atop the gate, which is spiked—more as a formality than as a threat. However, to me, they do seem threatening.

"This is it," says Daddy from the driver's seat. "No turning around now."

Mama's concentration is glued to the gate. "I'm ready. How about you, Lexi?"

My nerves rattle like pinballs aiming for a high score. "Ready."

"Here we go," says Daddy.

He rolls down his window and presses the intercom button.

"Flinder residence," a formal man's voice answers.

"My name is Tony Prost. My family and I are visiting here in town, and we have some very important information for Mrs. Flinder."

A pause. The man's voice sounds more cautious. "What type of information?"

"It's about her family. We need to talk to her in person. It's a bit of an emergency."

A longer pause. Then a buzz follows and the gate door swings open. "Please proceed," the voice says.

We ride in silence until we reach an alcove near the entryway. The mammoth house is a testament to the wealth of the Flinder family. A broad-shouldered man in a black pinstripe suit exits the front double doors and steps briskly to the car.

"Follow me," he says. "You may leave your vehicle parked here for now."

Mama glances back at me. I nod and smile reassuringly. We join Daddy and follow the well-dressed man into the house, passing a sprawling flowerbed of perfectly arranged white, red, and blue flowers inviting us with their enticing scents. We enter a vast foyer with a white marble floor, dark brown sitting chairs, and contemporary paintings.

"Please have a seat. Mrs. Flinder will be with you shortly," he says, before disappearing down the hallway.

Naturally, Daddy is the first to sit on one of the massive chairs. Mama and I stand together nervously. I force my arms to remain still at my sides, trying to keep my wrists apart. Daddy drums his fingers on the armrests and smiles, trying to put us at ease.

"Excited?" he asks.

"Nervous," says Mama.

I nod. "Me too."

"Take a deep breath," says Daddy. "Don't worry. It'll be fine. I'm here to run interference if you need it."

"Thanks," says Mama.

She reaches out and squeezes my hand for reassurance.

"I can't wait to meet her," I whisper.

Before Mama can respond, the click—click—click of high heels on the marble floor resonates from the hall. Daddy bolts to his feet and takes his place beside us. We gawk collectively at the marvelous woman entering the foyer. The pictures from Daddy's laptop did not do her justice. Her queenly manner exudes power. When she smiles, her pearly teeth shimmer. She wears tailored black slacks and a silky blue blouse.

"Hello, I'm Cassandra Flinder," she says, her voice soothing yet assertive. "How can I help you?"

We stand in awkward silence, stunned. Daddy takes a timid step forward to introduce himself, but Mama suddenly reaches across and offers her hand.

"I'm Cindy," she says.

As they shake hands, I watch Mama's joy and Cassie's curiosity simultaneously. The handshake ends, but their gaze remains.

"This is my family," says Mama. "My husband, Tony."

"Nice to meet you," says Daddy, shaking her hand.

Mama motions to me. "And this is our daughter, Alexis."

"Hi, Alexis," my aunt greets me.

"Hi," I answer, waving at her. "You can call me Lexi."

She nods and then looks at Mama. "So, what can I do for you?"

"Actually, we have something to tell you," says Mama. "Is your husband here?"

"He is at his office working. Why? Do you need to speak with him instead?"

Mama holds up her hands. "No, no. Our message is for you only. We have traveled from Little Rock, Arkansas. I used to live here in Chattanooga with my mama when I was a young girl."

"Chattanooga is a wonderful city," says my aunt.

"Yes, I suppose it is," says Mama, focusing on the floor. "I didn't see any of its good qualities back then. My mama and I had to escape from my father. He was abusive."

Cassie appears startled by Mama's brutal honesty. "I'm sorry," she says.

Mama smiles. "It's in the past now. Besides, my mama did what she had to do to save me. I just found out recently that she tried to do the same for her other daughter."

Uneasiness flickers across Cassie's expression. "That's—well—it sounds like your family has had some hard times."

"More than you can understand," says Mama. "Maybe you knew my mama. Her name was Lisa James."

My aunt suddenly pales, as if she has traded bodies with a ghost. "What did you say your name was?"

"Cindy James," says Mama. "My sister's name is Cassie. Our mother, Lisa, had her baby taken away from her by her mother, Elaine, who gave the baby to Mr. and Mrs. Hunt, your parents. Cassie, you're my sister."

As Cassie's hands tremble, she hides them behind her back. I am sure that she is rubbing her wrists together. The shock of this announcement has had a visible effect on her. Without warning, her eyes grow wild and her cheeks redden.

"Get out of my house," she says, her teeth now unbecomingly bared.

Mama seems shocked. I watch Daddy and find the same bewilderment in his expression.

"But we're sisters," says Mama. "And Lexi is your niece. I have the journal writings from Grandma Elaine and our mama to prove it."

"How dare you enter my home and spread these lies," says Cassie. "I've never seen you, I don't know you, and we're certainly not family. Leave now or I'm calling the police."

Mama takes a step backward. "Cassie, please—"

"My name is Cassandra Flinder, and I'm married to the mayor." Her pitch rises. "I couldn't *possibly* be related to you. I don't want to see you again."

The suited man steps into view from around the corner. "Is there a problem, Mrs. Flinder?"

She glares at Mama. "No problem, Donovan. These people were just leaving."

"Would you like me to escort them out?" he asks.

Daddy pulls Mama away from Cassie. "That won't be needed, sir," he says. "We're going. Sorry for the misunderstanding."

Cassie folds her arms. "Enjoy your trip back to Little Rock," she says icily.

Mama is obviously distraught, but Daddy forces her to the door, with me close at their heels. We return to the car and leave the Flinder property in dazed silence.

Back on the main road, Mama finally speaks.

"I don't believe it." Her voice is dispirited.

"She knows," says Daddy. "It was all over her face. Somehow, she already knows about us."

Mama's lip quivers. "Then why did she respond that way?"

"Maybe she's afraid?" I say.

"Why would she be afraid of finding the rest of her real family?" says Mama.

Daddy drums his fingers on the steering wheel. "Because it's threatening."

I lean forward between the front seats. "What do you mean, Daddy?"

"Think of the family history: murder, a baby out of wedlock, and a track record of mental instability. The James women are a hotbed of scandal. What do you think information like this would do to her husband's chances to be elected as state governor?"

Realization sparks in Mama's expression. "She's protecting herself?"

"And her husband," says Daddy.

"So how will we know how she really feels?" I ask.

Daddy places a hand on Mama's arm. "I guess there's only one way to find out."

She nods. "We'll have to talk to her away from that house."

"How can we do that?" I ask.

Daddy smiles. "I've got a plan."

Cindy James

Our red Ford Taurus approaches another black gate protecting another extravagant estate.

"I'm getting tired of these gated communities with their intercoms and security cameras," says Tony with a grin. "Makes them feel like castles."

"Or prisons," I say.

"Nice," says Tony. He rolls down his window and lowers his voice. "Let's try door number two."

He presses the intercom button, and we hold our breaths.

"Yes?" says an elderly woman's voice.

"Hello, I'm Tony Prost, and I'm here with my family. We were wondering if we could have a few minutes of Mr. and Mrs. Hunt's time."

"How do you know the Hunts?"

Tony focuses on the security camera. "We know their daughter, Cassie."

With a buzzing sound, the gate opens.

"Please drive in," says the woman's voice.

Lexi reaches forward and clutches my hand as we move toward the colossal house.

***

Five minutes later, the three of us sit on a plush green couch across from Jeffrey and Christina Hunt, seated in matching burgundy armchairs side by side. Timid, observant Lexi is wedged between Tony and me. The scent of fresh coffee, usually comforting, does little to calm my nerves. I quickly scan the living room's expensive décor—a Victorian style grandfather clock, a double-sided stone fireplace centered between the living and dining rooms, several paintings depicting famous cities from around the world, and a massive Persian rug beneath our feet that must have cost what I make for a year's salary.

Finally, I focus on Christina, whose frail figure struggles to maintain perfect posture. Dressed in casual black slacks and an embroidered purple sweater with a flower design, her salty-white hair is permed and precise. Jeffrey's blue jeans and green golf shirt belie his wrinkled face. In spite of their youthful attire, they both appear to be ancient. Because Grandma Elaine's journal mentioned several times that these pleasant-looking people were a decade younger than she and her husband, Paul, Christina and Jeffrey must be close to ninety by now.

"So, you mentioned that you knew our Cassie," says Christina, her voice graceful.

"We appreciate your allowing us into your home," I say, trying to sound genteel. "This may come as a surprise to you, but my name is Cindy James. I'm the daughter of someone you once knew, Lisa James. My grandma was Elaine, a friend of yours."

Christina flinches. She sets her coffee on the end table beside her. "Oh my," she says.

Jeffrey interlocks his fingers and focuses on the floor, seeming to journey back in time.

"This is my husband, Tony, and my daughter, Alexis," I say, swallowing a lump in my throat. "We've come from Little Rock, Arkansas, because we recently learned about my connection to Cassie. I never even knew she existed until yesterday. My Grandma Elaine wrote about taking Cassie from her mama—*my* mama—Lisa, and giving her to you to raise as your daughter."

Christina's hands quiver. She tries to steady them against the armrests of her chair. "Your mother was Lisa?" she asks.

I nod. "I want to ask you, face to face, if it is true. Did my Grandma Elaine give Cassie to you?"

She stares at me, petrified. Then her expression changes to one of relief, as if she can finally release a burden she has been carrying for decades.

"Yes. Cassie's real mother is Lisa, and Elaine brought her to me one night and made me promise to keep it a secret. Does Lisa want to see Cassie?"

Tears burn my eyes. "Lisa passed away from cancer almost thirty years ago."

Christina glances away. "I'm so sorry."

I bite my lip. "According to the journal she left for me, she came back to get Cassie at one point, but she wasn't allowed to see her."

She swallows hard. "I'm sorry. I thought it was best at the time. I didn't want to lose Cassie. You have to understand—"

"I understand, Mrs. Hunt," I say, extending my hands in a peaceful gesture. "I'm not upset about that. I know why you did that. What you may not know is that Lisa found a way to see Cassie for a short time."

She sighs. "I know."

"You knew?" I stammer.

"Yes. I had my suspicions when Nancy would bring Cassie home from shopping in town, and Cassie would cry for hours. Cassie kept saying 'Mama,' but whenever I tried to pick her up, she screamed and asked for 'Mama.' I finally confronted Nancy about it, and she confessed. I stopped her from taking Cassie to see Lisa. I didn't want to be replaced. I didn't want Cassie to love her real mother more than she loved me. It was terrible, I know. I'll never forgive myself for that."

A painful silence passes. Both of us are on the verge of tears.

"My mama wanted me to find Cassie and tell her the truth," I say. "I would have come much sooner, but I didn't discover the journal until this week. I realize that Cassie has a life of her own now, but she needs to know. She's family."

Christina gives Jeffrey a wary glance. "I don't think that's a good idea."

My right hand twitches, so I slide it under my leg. "We've already talked to her earlier today."

"You have?" she says, startled.

I nod. "We visited her and told her what we just told you, but she was angry and asked us to leave. I was hoping you could invite her here, so we can discuss everything. You are the only ones who know what really happened, and you can confirm our story to her. Surely she'll believe you if you tell her the truth. Please, Mrs. Hunt. This is a crucial part of my family history. She's the only sister

I'll ever have. I just want to know her and for her to know me and my family. Will you help us?"

Jeffrey stirs with agitation. "It's impossible," he says, his voice dejected.

"Why?" I ask.

He glowers at me. "Her husband, Victor, the mayor, won't allow it."

Tony leans forward. "What do you mean? Does he already know about us?"

Jeffrey shrugs. "I don't know, but if he finds out, things could get worse. That's the sort of information that could be threatening to his career."

"Things could get worse?" asks Tony. "How so?"

Jeffrey sighs and reaches to grasp Christina's hand, as if to console both of them. "I made a terrible mistake years ago. When Cassie first came to us, I was young and ambitious. I wanted to become politically powerful. Sam Flinder, Victor's father, was the mayor of Chattanooga at the time. I envied Sam. In my attempt to connect with the Flinder family and draw upon their influence, I courted their family while Cassie was growing up, preparing them for an arranged marriage that would benefit both families. Victor, who I was sure would be mayor someday in his father's footsteps, needed a wife from a prominent family, and I thought I needed the benefits of such an alliance."

Tony crosses his arms. "So you *forced* Cassie to marry Victor?"

Jeffrey's body stiffens. "I didn't force her, but I made it clear what our preference was and what hers should be as well."

I lean forward toward Christina. "Mrs. Hunt, how did you react to this?"

She swallows hard. "I was in favor of it because I wanted to make sure my daughter was provided for. Neither of us could have imagined how it would turn out."

Suddenly, Lexi interjects. "What happened? What went wrong?"

The Hunts stare at Lexi, as if they hadn't noticed her before now. Christina smiles sadly.

"Cassie married Victor as planned, but it wasn't long before we found ourselves shut out of her life."

"How so?" I ask.

Jeffrey pounds his thighs with his fists. "Victor controlled her, dominated her. Where she went, whom she talked to, what she said—he monitored it all. When he became mayor, there was immense pressure for them to be a perfect couple. Cassie told us she was miserable, constantly worried, and afraid she would make a mistake that he would punish her for. She said Victor was dealing with dangerous people, and the stress caused him to behave erratically. We were concerned that she was being abused. Soon, she wasn't allowed to see us anymore. Victor manipulated her and kept her on a tight leash. His father, Sam, passed away unexpectedly—his death is still a mystery, but we are sure that Victor caused it. After that, Victor took over the family estate and the Flinder's assets. He's power-hungry and ruthless. For several years, we've barely seen Cassie or spoken to her."

"Why doesn't she leave him?" asks Tony.

Jeffrey sighs. "If only it were that easy. Victor has threatened her on multiple occasions, and he has influence with the local law enforcement, so it's an impossible situation. If Cassie tries to get help or we try to intervene, Victor will hurt her, maybe even *kill* her. He's not a stable man, and we can't risk our daughter's safety, or Lucy's, for that matter."

Lexi perks up. "Who's Lucy?"

"Cassie's daughter," says Christina. "She's eighteen, but she's not—well—she's not—doing well."

Lexi marvels. "She's *my* age."

Christina nods. "She looks a little like you too, except her hair is bright red. We worry about her. Finding out about all of this could be very upsetting for her."

We all sit silent as we reflect on our shared history, which has opened up like an old wound. Jeffrey rubs his hands together.

"Now you see why we can't ask Cassie to come here. We haven't seen her in over a year. She told us that Victor tracks her cell phone, so it isn't safe for her to call us. From time to time, she sends us letters to give updates on herself and Lucy. Other than that, we have no contact with our daughter and granddaughter."

More silence. Christina finally rises and stands before us. She addresses me sincerely.

"Cindy, I want to tell you how sorry I am that I turned away your mother when she tried to see Cassie. It was a selfish, heartless thing for me to do, and I hope she was able to forgive me. Now, after all these years, I understand what she was feeling—the pain of losing a daughter, not being able to spend time with her, having to miss making memories. Will *you* forgive me?"

Her bony hand grasps mine and squeezes with surprising strength. My throat swells with emotion.

"I forgive you," I say. "I'm sorry about Cassie."

"Thank you," she says, relieved. "I realize it is a lot to ask, but if you could help Cassie and Lucy, I would be grateful. They are in a desperate situation. Maybe you can find a way to free them from Victor's control."

I am overwhelmed. "But I don't know what we can do."

"Find Lucy first," she says. "Maybe she can help you reach Cassie. Just be careful. Victor is powerful and dangerous."

I glance at Lexi and Tony. They seem supportive and determined. I look back at Christina.

"All right," I say, "where do we find Lucy?"

Lexi James

I wring my hands and take several deep breaths, trying to net the butterflies fluttering in my stomach. My jaw reflected in the hospital restroom mirror appears tense.

Your life is about to change. Try not to think about how huge this moment is. Easy does it. Just act normal.

Yeah, "normal," as if that's possible for you, Lexi Hexy.

Shut up! Keep your comments to yourself. This is a big day for me, so don't ruin it.

Don't worry about my ruining it. I'm sure you and your demented wrist rubbing, fingernail slicing, and eyebrow tearing will do the trick.

Get out of my head!

Mama steps to my side. She's wearing her I-will-become-a-mama-bear-and-kill-someone-to-protect-you-if-needed expression.

"How are you doing, Lexi?"

I shove my hands into my pockets to keep my wrists apart. "I'm ready, I guess."

"Are you sure you don't want help?"

I nod. "Positive. I need to do this alone. It will be best this way. Less pressure for her."

Mama places her arm around my shoulders and kisses my forehead. "I'm proud of you. I think things will get better once we can bring the rest of our family together."

"Me too, Mama."

Our faces reflected in the mirror reveal their sameness, the common understanding of our silent struggle. I have her nose, her ears, and her smile. But most of all, I have her eyes—those soul windows that want to close instead of open when I feel the poison in my mind. Yet, we both must keep our eyes open, watching out for each other. As we match gazes in the mirror, it's clearer to me than ever before that we need one another's strength to begin a new cycle.

If we have *any* chance to break the family curse, it begins now, with our standing together. Mama took a different path, trying to walk away from the self-destructive dysfunction of the women before us, but that way of living will only become a lasting legacy in our family if I follow in her steps.

"Daddy and I will be waiting outside, in case you need us," says Mama.

I smile. "Thanks."

She hugs me and leaves the bathroom.

I wait a few moments, staring into the mirror. Finally, I take my hands from my pockets and exit into the antiseptic empty hallway. The building feels like a sterile bubble, and it has that medicated smell that usually turns my stomach. Quietly, I seek the last room on the right and enter through the open doorway. The room scarcely has enough space for the small sink, narrow closet, two visitor chairs, hospital bed, and rack of medical equipment in the corner.

On the hospital bed facing the door sits an attractive red-haired young woman wearing a plain gray T-shirt and gray sweatpants, her legs propped against her chest, writing feverishly in a notebook. I notice her fair skin and bare feet. My insides twist in knots as I approach. Her face is covered with bruises and cuts. She seems absorbed in her own world as she concentrates on the page before her.

"Hi, Lucy," I say, trying to keep my voice soft.

No response. Only the sound of her pencil scribbling.

"Do you mind if I come in?"

More written words.

I step closer. My presence goes unnoticed as she continues to write. She scans the page as if on fast-forward skipping through scenes.

"My name is Alexis," I say, "but you can call me Lexi, like my family does. I'm a friend of your family from out of state, and you can trust me. It's nice to meet you."

She remains engrossed in her work. I offer a hand wave of greeting, but she does not glance up from the journal. I approach the visitor's chair next to the bed.

"Lucy, do you mind if I sit down?" I wait. Nothing. "I'm going to sit down now. If it bothers you, please say something."

After another mute moment, I ease myself down onto the chair. "Is it all right if we talk? I'm eighteen, just like you. I'm glad I can finally meet you."

I fold my hands in my lap and the silence of the room settles over me. The atmosphere is pleasant, undisturbed. Even the rapid rushing of her pencil on the paper creates a soothing effect. My body relaxes.

"Is that your diary, Lucy?"

She continues to write without acknowledging me.

"I like writing too," I say. "It helps me process things. A lot of women in my family have spent time journaling."

I lean to the right, trying to catch a glimpse of the page, but she has concealed it from view.

"So, what are you writing?" I ask, glancing away and expecting no reply.

Suddenly, the pencil pauses on the paper. I glance back at her and notice a twitch in her left cheek. She looks at me.

"Me," she says, her voice mild and sweet.

She focuses back on the journal. I consider her response for a moment. Doubt creeps in, and I wonder if I should leave. Fighting my nervousness, I feel compelled to give her a chance. Perhaps a different tactic might yield a different result. Involuntarily, my fingers tear at my eyebrows.

"Can I sit beside you on your bed?" I ask. "I promise I won't look at what you're writing. I just want to keep you company."

She lifts her pencil from the paper and points to a spot on the bed next to her. I move my fingers from my eyebrows and place my hands at my side. Swallowing a lump in my throat, I sit at her side. As I move, she tilts the journal away so I can't see it. We sit just a foot apart.

"I like it here," I say. "It's peaceful. A lot quieter than out there."

Her fingers lower the pencil into the binding of the journal. "You shouldn't have come," she says.

Suddenly, she tears a page out of the journal, making me flinch. Then she snaps the book shut and shoves both the page and the journal under her pillow. Without focusing on me, she changes her pose to sit Indian-style and places her hands, palms up, on her knees. Only now do I notice the brush-burn-like marks on her wrists. She continues to stare at the far wall.

"Lucy, can I tell you a secret?" I whisper.

Her head drops and rises in a quick, fluid motion. I finally realize that she has nodded "yes."

"I rub my wrists too," I say. I extend my hands and turn my palms up, parallel with hers. The reddened, raw skin on our wrists is nearly identical. "It's something that runs in my family."

Her brown eyes lock onto mine. "My family too. My mother and me."

I smile. "I know. I saw her do it earlier today."

I wait for her to be shocked, but she glances away and focuses on the far wall again. Her voice is scarcely audible. "I know why you're here, Lexi."

The butterflies in my stomach resume fluttering. "You do?"

Her head nods again. "You shouldn't have come. Your being here in this room right now will change everything. Did my mama make you leave?"

I fidget on the bed. "Yes. How did you know?"

Her hand reaches to touch mine. "Have you come to rescue me? Do you think I'll leave with you?"

"I—I wasn't sure. How do you know about me?"

She releases my hand and smiles a secretive smile. "We sent the letter."

"What?"

"The letter from Grandma Lisa to your mama in the pink envelope. My mama has had it hidden for years. It's been our secret. We had to wait for the right time to send it." She touches her wrists together without scraping them. "I can't explain everything now. We're not safe."

I stare at her bruises. "Did your daddy put you here?"

She nods. "I can't be trusted. I'm unpredictable and unstable. I'm a sleepwalker in the worst way. Just like my mama. I had to be punished. That's what he said."

She gives me a pained expression.

"If your daddy did this to you, why didn't he go to jail?" I ask.

Lucy tilts her head to one side. "He framed someone else for it. That's what he does. He has control over everyone. I don't fit in.

I don't belong with him and my mama. They are the perfect family without me, he says. I'm not normal."

"I think you're perfectly normal," I say.

She bites her lip. "What did you say?"

"I said I think you're perfectly normal."

"Say it again."

"You're perfectly normal."

Her tears well up. "I wish I were. I really do. Lexi, you have no idea how twisted this gets."

"What do you mean?"

She presses her palms against her forehead. "I'm trapped here. If I try to leave, or if Mama tries to help me escape, he'll track us down and hurt us. Daddy is going to find out you visited me. Somehow. He always knows. You aren't safe now. Please go home before something happens. You shouldn't have come."

I shake my head. "We're not leaving. We're going to help you escape."

Lucy tucks her hands under her legs. "You really want to help?"

"Of course," I say.

She sighs. "Mama and I have known about you and my Aunt Cindy for a long time. We've just been waiting until we needed to send the letter, just like Grandma Lisa instructed. I'm sorry we sent it, because we've put you in danger, but we didn't have any other choice."

"Why not?"

"Because my daddy's going to kill me," she admits tearfully.

My stomach lurches. I place a hand on her arm. "Nothing's going to happen to you."

She flinches. "He's already planning it. I'm a liability, he says. I need to go away, he says." She points to her battered face. "This was just a taste of what's coming. It will help him become governor if I have an unfortunate accident. He'll have people's sympathy once I'm gone."

"That's ridiculous, Lucy. Why do you think that?"

Her countenance grows murky. "He told me."

"Your daddy told you?"

She shakes her head and holds a finger to her lips. Before I have time to respond, her hand slides under the pillow and retrieves the torn sheet of paper from her journal. She crinkles it into a ball and drops it into my hand.

"I'll need your phone number," she says.

She picks up her journal and pencil and asks me to write my number. The word *ESCAPE* is written over and over on the page.

"See you soon," she says.

She motions toward the door with her pencil. Reluctantly, I climb off the bed and make my way to the door.

"Goodbye, Lucy," I say.

"Goodbye, Lexi," she says, without glancing up.

I step into the hallway and close the door behind me. After un-wrinkling the paper wad, I read the scribbled note.

Entrance of Forest Hills Cemetery tomorrow at noon

Cindy James

We arrive at Forest Hills Cemetery fifteen minutes early because I couldn't wait any longer. The entrance consists of tall, rectangular stone pillars on either side of the paved path. A stone wall stretches from the far side of each pillar, forming the outer barrier of the cemetery. As we pass the pillars, we view the variety of trees spread among the gravestones, their plentiful branches creating a dazzling canopy of leaves with multiple shades of green. Under different circumstances, I might find this setting peaceful.

We park on the path near the entrance and soberly view the gravestones. Tony and Lexi exit the car and stand together chatting, while I pace, my hands shaking, my head throbbing. I check my watch a few times every minute until noon arrives.

Tires squeal on the asphalt drive near the cemetery entrance. A classy white Cadillac pulls behind our red sedan, its tinted windows concealing the occupants. Tony and Lexi huddle beside me, either seeking protection or offering it. The driver's door opens, and my sister steps out, wearing a navy blue business suit and a stressed expression. She walks toward us.

"I'm alone," says Cassie.

"What's going on?" I ask.

She doesn't seem to process my question. "Does anyone know you're here?"

I shake my head. "No."

Cassie smiles at Lexi. "Lucy likes you. She wouldn't have talked to you if she didn't."

Lexi fumbles her hands together. "What happened to her? What did your husband do to her?"

Cassie's cheek slightly twitches. "All you need to know right now is that you're not safe. I'm glad you are here, but it was a mistake to come. I was desperate, so I sent Mama's letter to you, but it was selfish of me. I'm sorry."

"I don't understand," I say.

Tears glisten on her lashes. "I'm risking my life *and* Lucy's by being here with you. I had to plan a fake event in town as a decoy so I could come today." She points to the white Cadillac behind her. "This isn't even my car. I borrowed it from a friend. My real car has a GPS tracker on it, so my husband can trace my movements. I drove my car to the fake event, left it there, and came in my friend's car. As you can tell by now, it's not safe for me to be seen with you. So please don't take this lightly. There is much more going on than you realize. To use Lucy's favorite word, the situation is 'twisted.'"

Tony takes a step forward, his demeanor in fix-it mode.

"What can we do to help?" he asks.

Cassie averts her gaze. "Nothing. My husband, Victor, is a powerful man. He has done some things that I'm ashamed of. He plans to kill Lucy in a few days and make it look like an accident. That's why I had to send the letter, so you could find us. But now I've endangered you as well."

I place a hand gently on her shoulder. "How do you know Victor plans to kill Lucy?"

She gives me a sad smile. "As I said, it's twisted. I'm close to someone who works for Victor. He heard about the plan, and he warned me several weeks ago."

"Who is he?" I ask, withdrawing my hand.

She speaks guardedly. "It's not important right now. I just want to say that I'm sorry I had to act the way I did yesterday when we first met. I was dying inside to hug you and tell you how I've been waiting for years to see you, but I knew Victor was listening. The whole house is bugged. So is my phone. I have to be a different person around him, always watching what I say, how I say it, and whom I talk to. After you left the house, I erased the tape recording—something I've never done before—to make sure he didn't find out about you. When he came home and tried to watch the tape, he asked me why he couldn't see or hear anything. I told him it must have been a faulty tape. It took a while to convince him. It wasn't easy. I hope you can understand how complex this situation is."

I embrace her. "We're going to help you and Lucy escape."

As I step back, she changes from being thrilled to being terrified. Before she can reply, Tony speaks firmly.

"Cindy's right. We're not leaving without you and your daughter."

I nod. "You are family, Cassie. That's all there is to it."

She bites her lip and steps away from us. "Thank you. You can't imagine what your support means to me after all these years of having none. But I can't accept it. It was wrong of me to bring you here, and I won't keep you in danger just to help myself. I know Mama wanted you to save me, but it's impossible."

"Cassie, wait—" I plead.

"No," she says, raising her hands resignedly. "Please don't make the situation harder than it is. There's no fixing this. I even told Mama that when she visited."

"She visited you? When?"

"I don't have time to explain. Victor will be looking for me soon. I came to say 'goodbye' and to give you this." From her pocket, she hands me a folded, smudged paper. "From Mama," she says. "It will clear things up."

"Please, let us help," I say, becoming desperate.

She backpedals toward the car. "Goodbye. Take care of yourselves and please go back home before it's too late."

I try to follow her, but Tony restrains me.

"Let her go," he whispers. "Let her go."

I watch Cassie leave, my heart pulsing with pain. The Cadillac turns and leaves the cemetery. The hum of the engine disappears in the distance, leaving us in silence. Lexi grasps my hand.

"We're not going home, right?" she asks, more as a statement than a question.

"No," I say, "not until they come with us."

Tony leads us back to the car, smiling. "I was both afraid and hoping you'd say that."

***

Lexi and Tony are watching the motel TV, giving me privacy after we returned from the cemetery. Seated on a warped wooden picnic table just beyond the parking lot, I turn the smudged paper over and over. Ancient voices whisper in my consciousness.

Cindy, it's been such a long time since we've talked. So nice of you to allow me back into your thoughts. I've missed our madness together.

Not now. Please, just leave me alone. I have to read this letter.

You know what this trip is, don't you? A new can of family worms. And you're getting ready to open it all the way. Watch those wicked vermin spill all over your husband and daughter. My, my, you have a knack for finding messes to heap on yourself and those around you, especially when those messes don't want to be found.

I need to rescue my family. I need to save them, like Mama asked. This letter is the next step toward that goal.

Stupid, Cindy. You need to run away. It's not worth fighting for lost family members who are as damaged as you are. Don't read that letter. The darkness is going to consume you and Lexi anyway. Why bring Cassie and Lucy, two more cursed lives, into the fold?

Let go of me! Get out of my thoughts. I'm reading this letter and that's final.

It'll just be another poison to ingest. Trust me. You've got twisted roots in your family tree. Better cut and run why you still have the chance.

I open the letter, smoothing the grainy paper in my trembling hands. After wiping tears on my shirtsleeve, I clench my teeth and prepare for the worms to fall where they may.

Dear Cassie and Cindy,

This may be the last letter I will ever write. Cancer is carving me up from the inside. I've known about the disease for months, but sometimes it takes the reality of impending death to realize what you should have done in your life.

I have two beautiful daughters whom I love more than life itself. You do not know each other yet, but someday you will, and I wish I could be there for that reunion. I'm entrusting both this letter and another letter in a pink envelope to Cassie. Cassie, I will leave it to you to send your sister the letter in the pink envelope when you think the time is right, when you need rescuing more than you need to stay hidden. Cindy, I've made many poor choices, but this isn't one of them. You will understand my reasoning soon.

I'm writing this letter sitting in my rental car in the parking lot of a hotel in Chattanooga. Cindy, you'd be proud of me for finally mustering up the guts to travel. You're living your dream in Kansas City, and I couldn't be prouder. As much as I've missed you, your absence has given me plenty of time to travel back and forth to see Cassie in secret. Now both my daughters have had the chance to know their mama.

Cassie, as we discussed earlier today, once you give this letter to your sister, you need to set up a time to find what else I buried. I hope you will remember exactly where I told you to look on the mountain. Please understand that some family secrets can be disastrous if shared at the wrong time, or divine if shared at the right time. The specific timing will be your choice.

I want you two to be happy, and I want you to have daughters of your own to love and cherish. I hope it will not be long before you are able to find each other. That is a hope not even your Grandma Elaine could smother.

Love always,
Mama

P.S. *Hurry to Lookout Mountain and use the dates on Grandma Elaine's grave.*

A shorter note is scribbled at the bottom of the page in different handwriting.

P.P.S. *Cindy, meet me by the campfire ring on Lookout Mountain where you used to escape, tomorrow at noon. Mama was always watching out for you, even when you didn't think she was. She wanted me to tell you that. When you come tomorrow, bring a shovel. Cassie*

I grip the letter tightly in my hand. I had expected to shed tears, but instead a fire rises within me. It is now 1 p.m., so I leave the picnic table and walk back to our room, wondering how quickly the next twenty-three hours can pass.

***

The sun looms high overhead as noon arrives on the mountain. I stand on a mixture of rock and dirt, but my mind flows back to memories of a little girl seeking refuge on this craggy haven, away from Daddy, away from his fists, away from Mama's screams. Finding myself at the cleft of a rock, in the exact same position where my thirteen-year-old self once stood, seems surreal. The city of my haunted nightmares, Chattanooga, lies below, connected to a history I've struggled hard to reconcile.

My sweating, shaky hands nearly lose their grasp on the shovel. Part of me longs to call out for Mama, beckoning her to climb the mountain and join me where she can be safe from the man she married, free from her hellish life, but she is gone, and I am alone.

The peak beneath my feet is far from the tourist attractions of Lookout Mountain—Ruby Falls, the 145-foot high underground waterfall within the mountain, Rock City, famous for its bizarre rock formations, trails, and gardens, and the Incline Railway, a track with trolley-style cars climbing through the postcard-worthy scenery. Mammoth trees surround me on all sides, stretching their thick, leafy branches toward heaven. Patches of moss collect between rocky crevices and on the underside of jumbled stones. A steel campfire ring sits a few paces away, its interior lining blackened from scores of evening fires, creating a contrast with the pile of white ashes gathered on the ground within it. The lack of footprints in the dirt indicates the sparse visitor traffic, the very reason I used to visit this isolated spot.

I hear the rustling sound of footsteps echoing from the trodden grassy path nearby. The path winds all the way to the main road circling up the mountain. My red Ford Taurus sits parked in a ditch beside the intersection of the grassy path and the main road, making it easy for Cassie to find.

A beautiful woman, no longer adorned in upper-class attire, trudges into view, wielding a scuffed shovel. Wearing a white T-shirt and blue jeans splattered with dried orange paint, she stops within two feet of me. She surveys my green Capri pants and red University of Arkansas T-shirt and nods. As we grip our shovels, we can't quite believe what is happening.

"Hi," says Cassie.

"Hi," I say.

"Sorry for all the misdirection yesterday," she says. "The situation is delicate, so I have to do a lot of pretending, just to make sure I'm not being followed or watched. Does that make sense?"

I nod. "Perfect sense."

We stand and stare at each other until two wry smiles appear.

"Mama would have loved this," she says, motioning with her head toward the shovels.

I can't stifle a giggle. "Only a James women reunion would involve shovels and secrets." I survey the campfire ring nearby. "I guess we'd better start digging."

Without warning, Cassie drops her shovel and throws her arms around my neck. She leans her head against mine in total dependence, the same way Lexi used to do as a child when she was ill. Her embrace is so strong that I struggle to breathe.

"I'm sorry," she whispers. "I've just needed my sister all these years, and now you're finally here."

I encase her like a protective cocoon. "It's okay, Cassie. It's going to be all right from now on. I'm going to take you away from here. I'll make sure you're safe."

Her entire body seems to decompress, wilting with relief. As I support her, she weeps on my neck. When the emotion passes, she steps away and wipes her cheeks dry.

"Sorry. I'm a crier. Not in public, of course. Victor wouldn't have that. I've been holding tears back my whole life."

I give her a knowing smile. "Ready to burst?"

She runs a hand through her tousled hair. "Ready to escape."

"Come on," I say, hoisting my shovel. "We have some of our past to unearth."

"Follow me," she instructs.

I watch as she measures out seven paces from the right of the campfire ring and inserts the shovel blade into the hard ground. I join her and begin digging.

"Did you see anyone on the trail?" I ask.

"Not a soul."

"Good. We'll have to make this quick. Do you think you were followed?"

Cassie jostles the rocky dirt loose and moves a pile to the side. "I booked another fake appointment downtown, left out the back exit, and circled the city twice before coming. I think I'm in the clear."

"Let's hope we both stay that way."

We form a small hole, finding the soil a worthy opponent. Several minutes pass as we grind, scoop, and fling in alternating rhythms. The temperature seems to increase. The mountain is quiet, except for the sound of our tools. I notice that it is 12:20 p.m., so I quicken my pace. Cassie and I are lost in our thoughts as we excavate, digging almost three feet down after another twenty minutes.

Suddenly, my shovel dings against a solid object. We carefully clear away the dirt from the edges of a metal box the size of a small suitcase.

"Pirate treasure?" she asks, smiling.

"Here's hoping," I say, matching her grin for grin.

Gripping either side of the box, we raise and set it beside the newly formed crater. The lid is held shut by a combination lock with eight digits.

"I've been waiting for this for twenty years," says Cassie, bending down to scroll the numbers on the lock.

"I'm surprised you've waited this long," I say. "You've never wanted to come here and dig it up yourself?"

She glances at me playfully. "I wanted to every day, but Mama made me promise not to do it until you were with me. And when Mama makes you promise something—"

"You keep that promise," I say.

We smile, as if finishing each other's sentences is something we have always done.

"So what's the combination?" I ask, crouching beside her.

Cassie shrugs. "Mama never gave me a number to use. Did she ever give you one?"

I shake my head. "No, never."

"Hmm," she says. "What about the letter?"

I wipe my sweaty hands on my jeans and take the paper from my pocket. We scan it for a clue.

"Her last line," she says, "that's it."

"I was thinking the same thing. *'Hurry to Lookout Mountain and use the dates on Grandma Elaine's grave.'*"

She taps her finger on the box. "When was Grandma Elaine born and when did she die? What dates are marked on her grave?"

I squint, trying to conjure the image of the tombstone. "1913 to 1976."

She scrolls the eight numbers in sequence, and with a push on the lock, a metallic click echoes. Together, we pry open the lid. Inside lay at least two dozen stacks of rubber-banded $100 bills. A note is attached.

Congratulations, girls, you've found your inheritance. Grandma Elaine wanted to make sure you were both provided for. Despite her flaws, that's something I can remember about her with love. Split the money evenly and use it to better your lives. I'm sorry I couldn't give it to you earlier. Cassie, I knew Victor would find it and steal it from you. It was only safe for you to have it if you were planning to escape. Cindy, I knew you'd probably destroy it, just like I assume you will get rid of everything associated with the mansion (expect the chess set, I hope). Maybe enough time has passed to change your mind. Remember, not everything passed down through our family is evil.

You two are in charge of changing things. Share your stories with each other. Never stop communicating. It's the only way to start breaking the cycle of the James women. Love each other, and I will always be with you.
Mama

    We look at each other through mutual tears.
    "I miss her," she whispers.
    I place a hand on her shoulder. "Me too, Sis."
    She rests her hand on mine. "This is what she wanted—for us to find each other. I wish she could be here to see us together."
    I swallow hard. "She *is* here."
    Cassie nods and smiles. She gestures toward the metal case. "Can you keep this hidden for now? I have a plan to escape, but I'm still trying to figure out the timing."
    "Sure," I say. "How can we help?"
    She takes a deep, calculating breath. "Just wait for my signal. It will be a text message from Lucy from a disposable cell phone that Victor can't trace. It will be soon, maybe even today—" Her cell phone chimes, startling her. She picks up the phone and inspects the screen. "It's Victor. I've got to go. Can you take my shovel? I'll be in touch."
    "Don't you need to change?" I ask.
    "I brought dress clothes," she says. "I always have to be prepared. Just be ready for my signal, okay?"
    I nod and give her a farewell hug. She turns and runs back down the grassy path. After she is out of sight, I glance at the open metal box with the piles of green bills. I close the lid and relock it. I then scoop the dirt back into the gaping hole, removing the evidence of our earth-moving project.

***

As I pull the Taurus into the parking space by our motel room, I notice an unfamiliar black SUV two spots over. I have been keeping careful mental notes on the traffic around the motel, both persons and vehicles, so the black SUV immediately raises a red flag. Our door is closed and everything appears normal. I cover the metal case on the passenger seat with a travel map and walk to the motel door.

Before I can grasp the knob, the door swings open. A broad-shouldered man stands in the way, showcasing a politician's grin and wearing a flashy white suit with the corner of an orange handkerchief sticking out of the lapel pocket. His square jaw, fine black hair, piercing green eyes, and stately posture might make him seem handsome, even powerful, in another woman's estimation, but I know better. I recognize Victor Flinder immediately and distaste rises in my throat.

"Mrs. James, we've been waiting for you. Why don't you join us?" he says, his tone commanding. "We have a lot to discuss."

Victor extends his hand, as if he is a game show host inviting me to come inside to spin the wheel and win a prize. I glance past him at two imposing men with ruddy features, one bald and the other sporting spiky blonde hair. Each man wears a tan trench coat and stands in the living room, facing the couch on the back wall. Tony and Lexi sit side by side on the couch.

I enter the room and join them on the sofa. Victor closes the door and motions for the two burly men to give us privacy. As they nod and exit to the kitchen, the outline of a gun is visible under each of their coats.

Victor retrieves a chair from the kitchen table and sets it in the center of the living room. His movements are calculated and refined. He eases himself into the chair and crosses his right leg over his left knee. The politician's grin reappears.

"My name is Victor Flinder, and I'm the mayor of this fine city, but I'm sure you already know that by now. Do you happen to know what behavior is more disappointing to me than any other?" His question lingers unanswered. "Snooping," he answers. "Now, rumor has it—and my eyes and ears everywhere confirm it—that you three have been snooping all over my city for the past couple days, digging up things that should be left alone. This concerns me—no, this *worries* me. And when I'm worried, I don't sleep well, I don't eat well, I don't think well. There's only *one* thing I do well when I'm worried, and that is I make the worry go away."

He smiles and extends his hands as if to metaphorically embrace us. "You seem like nice, reasonable people. I appreciate your visiting my great city. I've worked hard to maintain its beauty and its mystery. To be honest, I'm interested in your welfare because the one thing I hate more than anything—snooping—is the kind of thing that turns decent folks into dangerous folks. Like a dog catching a scent. If this dog catches the wrong scent and follows it to its source, it could turn out that what the dog has been smelling has the power to harm it, even kill it. That would be terrible. Poor, dumb dog. It just wanted to dig up some dirt and find a tasty bone, but now it has swallowed poison, or has been caught in a metal trap which maims it for life, or has had its stupid head blown off."

Lexi flinches, and I grasp her hand.

"Mr. Flinder," says Tony, his voice calm. "We are simply on vacation. We haven't been doing anything illegal. We're sight-seeing."

Victor sighs and checks his watch, as if suddenly bored with our company. "Unfortunately, the tour of this city is over for you. I would strongly recommend you return home to Little Rock while your car still has gas in it, rather than all over it. I've heard horror stories about vehicles catching fire around here for no apparent reason. Spontaneous combustion, some people say. Others attribute it to the gasoline paint job someone gave the car before lighting a match to it. Who's to say? I just know it's an unsafe area of town, especially for out-of-towners. I wouldn't be a good mayor if I didn't warn you of the danger."

The insolence burning in my gut spikes to my throat and escapes before I can squelch it. "I'm sure Cassie is proud to have you as a husband."

His glare pierces my soul. Then, unexpectedly, his gaze softens and he chuckles. "I don't doubt it. She has always been attracted to power, and a mayor has that in spades. Well, *this* mayor, at least."

Lexi stirs, anxious to speak her mind, but I squeeze her hand as a warning. She stiffens and leans back against the couch.

"We appreciate your warning us about the danger," I say. "Tonight was our last night in town anyway. We've seen enough sights. Home is waiting."

I give him my sincerest expression, fear mixed with submission. He takes the bait and flashes his shark-grin.

"I'm glad we have an understanding," he says. "It would be a pity if we had to meet again."

"Agreed," says Tony. "Cindy, Lexi, why don't we start packing right now? No need to prolong our stay."

Lexi and I nod.

Victor smiles. "Excellent. My prediction was correct. You are indeed nice, reasonable people. Now, my friends and I will get out of your way so you can gather your belongings and depart while it's still daylight. It was a pleasure to meet you, and I trust you will have a pleasant trip home. Gentlemen, shall we go?"

The two gun-toting men reappear. Victor Flinder rises from his chair, winks at us, and then exits the room, with the men close at his heels. They slam the door with a jarring thud. It takes a few seconds for any of us to begin breathing again. Tony and Lexi stare at me, waiting. I rub my wrists together and lower my voice.

"We're leaving, but we're not going anywhere."

***

The mood in the car is tense as we pass a green sign on the highway announcing that we are thirty miles outside of Nashville. The skyline has darkened, causing the streetlights to buzz to life. Tony clutches the steering wheel with the intensity of an addict clinging to his last drug dose. Lexi has been quiet for the past hour, absorbed in her own thoughts. I sit, counting the miles, counting the minutes, and counting the number of car lengths between our car and the black SUV that has been tailing us since we left Chattanooga over two hours ago.

Tony checks the rearview mirror. "Still there."

"They haven't moved," I say. "Not very discreet. I guess they want us to get the message. I wonder if they're going to follow us all the way to Arkansas."

"Do you think Mr. Flinder is with them?" asks Lexi.

Tony shakes his head. "I don't think so. I can only see Brute One and Brute Two in the front seats, the mayor's muscle."

"I feel awful leaving Cassie and Lucy," says Lexi. "They're still trapped, and we just get to go home, back to our lives. I thought you said we weren't going anywhere, Mama. Did you change your mind?"

"No, Lexi. I didn't change my mind."

"Then what are we doing?"

"Waiting for a signal," I say.

"What signal?" asks Tony.

Suddenly, Lexi's cell phone buzzes.

"It's a text," she says, "from Lucy."

My skin feels prickly with anticipation. "What does it say?"

"It says, *'Go to the nearest Best Western. There's a reservation in Tony's name. Your room will be on the first floor at the rear of the hotel. Take your belongings, check in, go to the room, and wait for another text. More instructions to come. Don't text back. Not safe. Lucy.'*"

"Where's the nearest Best Western?" I ask.

"Three miles," says Tony. "We just passed a billboard."

"*That's* the signal," I say contentedly.

***

We arrive at the Best Western, hauling our luggage and the metal case with us. Tony has parked the car in an obvious spot in the front parking lot. As we cross the shiny white tile floor and check in at the front desk, I watch through the sliding glass doors as the black SUV rolls by.

"You'll be in room twelve on the first floor," says the female staff member.

"Thank you," says Tony. He hands her his credit card.

"That won't be needed, sir," she says.

He gives her a bewildered glance. "Pardon me? I don't understand."

She smiles. "It's been taken care of. Enjoy your stay." She pushes a room key card onto the polished black counter.

Tony pockets the card. "Thank you," he says.

"Our pleasure," she answers. Then she lowers her voice. "Your ride will be ready shortly."

We stare at her, stunned.

"What ride?" I ask, leaning against the counter.

Her expression is unflappable. "Your ride will be ready shortly. Don't be late. Now, if you'll excuse me, I have some obligations to attend to."

She clicks on the computer keyboard, ignoring us.

"Let's go," I say.

We carry our belongings around the corner to Room 12. We flick on the lights, lock the door, set everything on the floor, and sit together on the comfortable king-sized bed.

"So, what's the plan?" asks Tony.

"We wait for our ride, I guess," I reply.

Lexi places a hand on my knee, appearing to draw comfort from the contact. "Do you think Aunt Cassie set this up?"

"I'm sure she did," I say.

Tony stands and paces near the window's drawn curtains. He glances at his watch. "This cat-and-mouse stuff is killing me. Why can't we just pick up Cassie and Lucy and leave town? Why all the secrets and misdirection?"

"It's a delicate situation," I say. "Cassie and Lucy are wrapped up in Victor's world, and he's not going to let them go. We have to do this carefully. We'll only have one chance."

Lexi's phone buzzes. She reads the text aloud.

"'Grab your bags and go out the window *now*.'"

"Come on," I say, slinging my purse over my shoulder.

Tony opens the curtains and unlocks and opens the window. He helps us drag our luggage to the window. We drop them onto the soggy grass behind the hotel, then we crawl through the window one at a time. A black van with its headlights on sits nearby. Its lights flicker.

"I guess that's us," says Tony.

We hurry to the vehicle. The sliding door is open and a middle-aged, handsome man sits hunched in the doorway. His jet black hair matches his black pants and black lightweight jacket. A jagged scar runs across his left cheek.

"Mrs. Flinder sent me. Get in," he says.

Wondering if we are making a terrible mistake, I climb into the van. Lexi and Tony follow. We occupy the long middle seat. The interior of the van has an unpleasant, musty stench. The man hops into the driver's seat and lurches the van through the lot, passing the parked empty black SUV. We veer onto the main road.

My heart thumps. I grasp Lexi's hand, glad she is sandwiched between Tony and me.

"All you need to know is that I work for Mrs. Flinder," says the man, focused ahead. "You can trust me."

"Who are you?" asks Tony.

"My name is Peter."

"How are you involved in all of this?"

The man smiles. "Services are needed, and I provide them."

I lean forward. "What does that *mean?*"

"You can trust me," the man repeats. "Now, I suggest we ride in silence."

I lean forward to challenge him, but Tony gestures for me to stop. Begrudgingly, I wait quietly.

Five minutes pass before the cell phone on the van's dashboard chimes. Peter picks it up and examines the message. He smiles.

"Time to hide," he says.

Lexi James

For two hours, my stomach has been somersaulting as I sit between Mama and Daddy driving along a country road on the outskirts of Chattanooga. We enter a private dirt drive and snake our way into the woods beside a ranch-style house. Peter cuts the engine, flicks off the headlights, and climbs out. We follow him and wait beside the van. A white Cadillac car rolls into view.

"Right on time," says Peter, smiling.

The driver's door opens, and we see Aunt Cassie dressed to the nines in a dazzling turquoise evening gown. She appears exhausted, coming toward us with labored steps.

"Thank you, Peter," she says.

He nods and moves toward the front door of the house. "I'll give you a minute in private."

Once he is gone, Cassie exhales heavily. "I'm sorry for the run-around. Like Lucy says, the whole thing is—"

"Twisted," I say.

Cassie smiles. "Yes, twisted." She glances at Mama. "Thank you for trusting me enough to follow the strange instructions. By now, Victor's men are probably on their way here. He wasn't going to let you go home safely. That's not Victor's style. He ties up all loose ends, no matter what it takes."

My heart thuds.

"So he was going to have us killed anyway?" asks Mama.

Cassie nods solemnly. "Because Victor thinks you've made it back into town, he will contact Peter to help take care of the situation."

Daddy shakes his head. "I don't understand. Peter said he worked for you."

Cassie bites her lip. "He does, but he's supposed to work for my husband. It's complicated." She pauses and takes a deep breath.

"I have to sneak Lucy out of the hospital tonight. Meet me at the Forest Hills Cemetery entrance tomorrow morning at 7 a.m. I have to leave now, or I'll be late for a fundraising party with Victor. I'll see you soon."

Aunt Cassie and Mama embrace.

"See you soon," says Mama.

Cassie hurries to her car. Within moments, her Cadillac disappears into the darkness.

Minutes later, we step into the house with our luggage. It is furnished with only the bare essentials—a living room with one gray couch and a matching armchair, a bedroom with a full-sized bed and nothing more, an alley kitchen, and a bathroom off the living room.

"Not exactly five-star, but it's sufficient for what you'll need tonight," says Peter, standing in the middle of the living room with his arms crossed.

"Whose house is it?" asks Mama.

Peter grins. "Nobody's and everybody's. Depends on who needs it. It's a safe house."

"A safe house?" I say. "You mean the kind they use to hide witnesses?"

Peter nods.

"So you're a cop?" Tony questions.

Peter laughs. "Not exactly."

"What is it you really do?" asks Mama.

"I'm a cop, a doctor, a mortician, a grave robber—whatever I need to be. It's probably better if you don't know anything else. I'll be outside keeping watch."

Without waiting for our response, he turns and leaves. We glance at each other, wondering whether to be amused or alarmed.

"Who is this guy?" asks Daddy. He shoots Mama a wry grin. "Your sister has an interesting taste in men."

Mama gives a nervous laugh. "Let's just try to get some rest tonight."

***

In the space between sleeping and waking, I dream of ghostly women crowding around a gravestone. I imagine myself in the circle, holding their boneless hands, feeling their otherworldly electricity. I am one of them.

Out of the fog surrounding our horror-film circle, a red-haired young woman appears wearing a white jacket that pins her arms against her chest. With closed eyes, she stumbles toward us, whispering something to herself. I know it is Lucy, and I know she is sleepwalking, just like Great-Grandma Elaine used to do. Her creepy voice sends shivers down my spine. She repeats a single word over and over—"Escape."

After Lucy passes our ghostly circle and enters the misty other side, I wake screaming. Mama is patting my chest, trying to stop my hyperventilation. Daddy is holding down my shoulders to stop my thrashing.

"Shh," says Mama. "Shh. It's all right. Stop screaming. I need you to stop screaming."

My voice catches. I blink several times, trying to decide if I am awake or still in a nightmare. Mama wipes sweat from my forehead and smiles.

"It's 6:30 in the morning. Time for us to go."

I sit upright on the couch. A moment later, the front door swings open and Peter steps into the room.

"Your car is parked outside," he says. "I filled it with gas." He tosses a set of keys to Daddy. "Unfortunately, I won't be joining you. I have a job to finish. It's been a pleasure."

Before we can respond, he is gone.

***

We have been riding in silence for quite a while, lost in our own thoughts. Using Peter's hand-written directions, which we found on the dashboard, we made our way out of the woods onto a road leading to the Forest Hills Cemetery. The voices in my head are playing their wicked game of tennis again, volleying back and forth.

Lexi Hexi, this is where it all goes wrong. Do you really think you'll get away safely? Can't you hear the craziness rattling in your brain? Soon you'll be sleepwalking like your nut-job cousin, Lucy. No telling what kinds of things you'll do then, when you're asleep, when you're insane.

Shut up, Alexis. Keep your head straight. We're about to save the rest of our family. This will help us move on and break the family curse. Don't lose sight of what's important now.

Lexi Hexi, the only thing you're going to lose is your mind. You're cursed—doomed to destroy your life and haunt a graveyard like the rest of them.

Be quiet, Alexis. We're on this trip so we can change our family.

Don't be naïve. The closer you get to this darkness, the more it will consume you. The same wildness lurks in your blood—that part of you that wants to break down, lose control, and watch everything burn.

Daddy's voice breaks into my mental conversation. "We're here," he says.

"Stop rubbing your wrists, honey," says Mama.

I glance at my wrists, finding them raw and red. Until Mama mentioned it, I wasn't even aware that I had been scraping them together. Now I wince with pain.

Focus, Alexis. Get ready.

Forest Hills Cemetery appears on the right. My heartbeat accelerates. My palms start sweating. The nerves in my body tense, tightening like springs.

Daddy turns into the cemetery drive. The white Cadillac is waiting on the main path. We pull alongside, and Mama and Cassie roll down their windows at the same time.

"Did anyone follow you?" asks Cassie.

Mama shakes her head. "We're alone. Are you okay?"

My aunt smiles and glances over at Lucy in the passenger seat. Then she looks back at Mama. "We'll be fine once we get out of here."

"So what's the plan?" asks Daddy.

Cassie motions toward the road. "We get the hell out of Dodge."

"Sounds good," says Daddy, grinning. "I can lead if you want."

Cassie focuses on the road again. "That's fine. Lucy was wondering if Lexi could ride with us. She wants to chat."

I unlock the back door. "Sure!"

As I hurry to the Cadillac, I turn and smile at Mama, who seems excited as I am. Then I hop into the backseat, luxuriating in the feel of the leather seats.

"Hi, Lexi," says Lucy, turning to wave. Her smile is in beautiful contrast to the ugly bruises and cuts covering the rest of her face.

"Hi, Lucy," I say. "I've missed you."

She ruffles her bright red hair. "Have you done any sleepwalking lately?" she asks.

I blush, remembering my dream last night. "No, sorry."

She bobs her head as if in rhythm to a song only she can hear. "No worries. I always ask just to make sure. I'll get you sleepwalking soon enough."

Aunt Cassie smiles at us. "Shall we go, girls?"

We nod in unison. We follow the Taurus to the main road and take a left. The anticipation is palpable. In my mind, I imagine all of the James women standing together on Lookout Mountain, celebrating our reunion.

A ring tone sounds as we approach an intersection. Cassie digs through her purse and raises the phone to her ear.

"Peter? Are you okay?" Cassie turns to Lucy with dread. "We're on our way now. What?! Oh my God—"

The Taurus, about thirty feet ahead of us, enters the intersection. Suddenly, a large black SUV careens crossways directly toward Mama and Daddy. The vehicles collide head on with an explosion of metal and glass. The crash sends shock waves through my body. The car spins around 180 degrees to face us. Bile fills my mouth at the sight of Mama and Daddy flopping like crash test dummies in the front seats.

Cassie slams on the breaks and we lurch to a stop, whiplashing me against the front seat. I hear pitiful screams and finally realize they are coming from me.

Between my screams, I hear Cassie yelling, "Oh, God, oh, God!" The cell phone has fallen and lies lopsided in the cup holder. Peter's voice continues through the small speaker. Lucy has curled herself into the fetal position on the passenger's seat, burying her face in her hands. I grasp the door handle.

"Lexi, stay in this car!" yells Cassie. "Don't go out there!"

"But my parents!" I scream through my tears.

"Don't move!" she yells.

My entire body quakes. "I have to go to them."

Cassie shakes her head with authority. "Stay put!"

The black SUV rolls away from the wreckage. The front portion of the massive vehicle seems barely scratched. One of Victor Flinder's men, the brute with spiky blonde hair and a tan trench coat, leaps out of the passenger side, pointing a gun in our direction.

"Out of the car now!" he bellows. "Walk toward me."

Cassie places her hand on the gearshift.

"No, Mama," says Lucy, her voice trembling. "Don't do it."

Taking a deep breath, Cassie says, "Let's get out slowly. Don't make any quick movements."

The next few moments feel like slow motion as we exit the car and step toward the armed man. I dare to glimpse the wrecked Taurus. It appears half its normal size. Mama's head droops to one side, her face bleeding in several places. Her eyes are closed, and she appears to be in a deep sleep. Daddy lolls his head toward the side as if he is drunk. His mouth is open, but no sound comes out. A deep red gash from his right temple to the left side of his jaw looks like war paint. The front half of the car has compacted on them. The lower parts of their bodies appear crushed and pinned against the seats.

"Get in," the man orders. He opens the back door and keeps the gun trained on us as we slide inside. He turns to the burly, bald driver and says, "You know where to take them. Hurry the hell up. We don't want to piss him off any more than he already is. I'll clean this up."

The driver nods and speeds away from the intersection, back to what I assume is downtown Chattanooga. Cassie reaches over and grasps both of our hands. Her face, like mine, is soaked with tears.

"It's going to be okay," she whispers, her voice shaky.

"Shut up," says the driver. He touches a handgun on the center console.

"Where are you taking us?" asks Cassie.

"I said shut up!"

"Please, just tell us where we're going."

The driver smiles. "The boss wants to see you, Cassandra. It's time to punish your bad behavior. Now shut up, or else I'll put a bullet in these girls' heads."

Cassie grips our hands even tighter, and we ride in silence, while my gut aches with a pain I have never felt before.

Cindy James

I come back to consciousness as my baby is being forced into the black SUV at gunpoint. I try to make a sound, but tightness in my chest is too strong. Paralysis numbs my limbs. Agonizing pain travels up and down my body. The coppery smell of blood fills my nostrils. Below my waist, my mangled legs look like broken, bloody toothpicks.

I watch the SUV disappear from the intersection. Through the cracks in my window, I recognize the man with the spiky blonde hair walking toward us, his tan trench coat flapping in the breeze. I try to shield myself, but my arms remain motionless.

"T—T—Tony," I stammer. "Help—"

Tony stirs. His face has a ghastly, wide laceration across it. Blood seeps from the wound. He strains to speak, but remains mute. The gunman has arrived at my door. He sadistically grins and raises his gun.

Suddenly, I hear tires squealing. The gunman whirls around as a black van drives into the intersection. The driver's side window rolls down and a shot explodes from the van. The gunman returns fire, his shot ricocheting off the van's side mirror. Another blast erupts from the moving vehicle. The man stumbles backward against my window, his blood splattering the glass. A final gunshot resounds, throwing the man against the car. The van screeches to a stop, while the body slides down my door.

I check Tony for any sign of alertness, but he remains in a stupor, his mouth opening and closing with no sound. I hear footsteps crunching on glass, and Peter appears between the spider-web cracks in the window. His right eye is swollen shut, his lips are cut, his cheeks are swollen with deep purple bruises, and hideous slashes crisscross his skin. His shirt is ripped and bloodied.

After dragging the gunman out of the way, he leans against the car and struggles to pry open my door.

"Can you help me open it?" he says, his voice raspy.

"I—can't—raise my arms," I say.

"Move back as far as you can," he says.

I give him a helpless stare. "I can't move!"

His fist shatters the window, and glass fragments spray my face. Peter's hand—drenched in red—claws at the inside door handle. With a grunt, he inches open the door until there is enough room to see me clearly.

"Hold on, Cindy. I'm calling for help," he says, rummaging in his pocket for his cell phone.

"My—baby—she's gone," I say. Fresh tears burn like fire. "Lexi—they took Lexi!"

"I know!" he yells. His expression is etched with the same anguish I feel. "They took Cassie and Lucy too."

Pain chokes my lungs. "Where are they taking them?"

"I don't know, but I'm going to find them," he says resolutely.

"Please, I beg you, bring back my baby!" I scream, my heart careening in freefall.

He nods. "I will. I promise. I can't call the police. It's not safe. But I'm going to call someone to come for you. He'll be here soon. You can trust him. I'm sorry, but I have to go."

"Where are you going?"

"I'm going to follow the SUV. There's still a chance I can catch up to them. I have to save them. Lucy—she's my daughter."

I stare, dumbfounded, but by the time I find my voice, he is dialing his phone on his way back to the van.

THE END

The saga of the James women will continue…

About the Author

Eric Praschan lives in Missouri with his wife, Stephanie. He holds a B.A. in English and a M.A. in Theological Studies. He has been writing for more than 20 years, focusing on suspense fiction.

For more information, visit www.ericpraschan.com.